TEMPORARY PLANETS FOR
TRANSITORY DAYS

Poems of Mykol Ranglen
by Albert Wendland

D G STAR
BOOKS

Temporary Planets for Transitory Days © 2020 by Albert Wendland

Published by Dog Star Books
Bowie, MD

First Edition

Cover art: Bradley Sharp
Book design: Jennifer Barnes

Printed in the United States of America
ISBN: 978-1-947879-18-8
Library of Congress Control Number: 2020935498

www.RawDogScreaming.com

Table of Contents

Secrets Out of Time
(Editor's Introduction)

What do you say about an adventurer, a space traveler, a reclusive writer, a "man who loved alien landscapes," and an altogether mysterious individual—who's also a poet?

Little is known about Mykol Ranglen, the author of this collection of poems. People are familiar with his reputation as a writer and the finder of the third Airafane Clip (the one that produced Annulus, the ring-shaped habitat in space). But much of what's said of him is still just conjecture. We've seen how stories about the discovery of Clips take on near-mythic elaboration, so assertions about his life can hardly be trusted. For instance, the claim that he found the fourth Clip no one now seriously believes. And even his non-fiction essays are annoyingly elusive on his character and past.

Mykol Ranglen, who are you?

We know what interests him from his essays: the human diaspora into the galaxy, the ancient archaeology of the Airafane and Moyocks, the changing of society with the discovery of Clips, the growing differences in class and attitudes, environmental contamination of other planets, the nature of frontiers, the perception of the new, the wonders of space, encounters with "the sublime," and, of course, alien landscapes.

But he says nothing about the man *behind* these words. No formal interviews of him exist, no long lists of biographical facts. He's seldom seen at his known homes (and then only furtively). And even photographs or recordings of him seem contradictory or vague, as if some government override agency purposely works to keep him obscure and his secrets intact. Like an undercover agent, he's a man of shadows, and he'll vanish from a conversation with little warning or obvious good-bye (I've encountered that myself).

Indeed, in recent years, there's been no trace of him. He's known for long voyages into space, reputedly alone, so we assume he's somewhere traveling now, exploring, seeking, maybe encountering more of the majestic interstellar marvels he writes about. I hope he is. From all he's said it's clear he'd rather be "out there" than on one of our more crowded domestic worlds.

And his poems suggest he's disconnected from his era, maybe even from time itself—or perhaps he's too immersed in it. He writes as much about pre-spaceflight 20th-century Earth as he does our 22nd-century Confederation. He describes the long-dead Airafane and Moyocks as if he's seen their ancient civilizations. Some people even argue that different versions of him exist, that he's somehow been split by his exotic travels into different manifestations of himself, that we never see the "whole" or "real" Ranglen but just the latest incarnation flitting into existence.

Such speculations are too off-the-grid for this realistic editor, but legends of space are as popular now as they were before we left Earth (you can see this in his poems). Maybe people just find it endearing to make up stories about him. Or, since we know he's read old science fiction, he intentionally fools the gullible by playing strange visitor from another planet, or a time traveler loaded with secrets.

His story has no tidy conclusion.

We *can* deduce, from guesses based on his writings, that he grew up on Earth and traveled in North America, that he studied its history of popular culture and pulp fiction, that he's familiar with geological and historical sites both on Earth and throughout space, that he's interested in 200-year-old "graphic narratives" (or comic books), that he's a scholar of Airafanology, that he's reviewed the ancient folklore and myth-making of various cultures, that he's explored landscapes on planets outside Confederation boundaries, and that, clearly, he's been in love, and more than once. For someone who emulates a loner lifestyle, he's been haunted by close—or desired—relationships.

However, all those connections to people, obviously to several women and to at least one child (apparently), plus his other ties to history, outer space, old writings, Homeworld, Annulus, and of course Earth, do not prevent his works from exuding a personal alienation and aloneness. He seems "in hiding."

Which brings us to the poetry collection before you.

In these poems we get actual names of people and places. We're not certain if the people are imaginary, or, if they do exist, whether Ranglen really encountered them or not. But a raw emotion often shows through, breaking his façade of separation. These poems are not as developed as those in his more well-known publications, not as "cosmic," but, though simple—and maybe because so—they might be closer to the truths of his life. Perhaps the names that appear here (Mylia, Alchera, Riley, Abby) refer to living people and actual places. We know at least one person mentioned *is* real, "Mileen," who's surely the talented e-painter Mileen Oltrepi. There's strong evidence she was Ranglen's close friend (or lover) before her apparent death in a meteorite explosion that accompanied the finding of the fifth Clip. And some places mentioned in the poems do exist on Old Earth or Homeworld, like Death Valley, Las Vegas, Weirton (West Virginia), and the Great South Desert.

But even though these references are provocative, we have no proof they refer to real events. And I remind readers that novelists and poets are perfectly capable of creating imaginary people, with lives. It's their job.

As for dating the poems, the style of tumbling free verse and sporadic rhymes (Ranglen counts only stresses, when he counts anything) grounds them in the writing habits of the last decade or two. They obviously come from an earlier time than the more sophisticated, and, in my opinion, more difficult and thus less rewarding later poems. What we have here are quick jottings, with just small amounts of after-thought or rewriting, where topics shift across planet and era. Most writers travel farther in their minds than they do in reality, but—who knows?—given Ranglen's reputation as an interstellar voyager, he might be an exception.

We'll never be certain.

As for how these poems came to be published, they're the result of a chance meeting between myself and the author. He already had a reputation as a withdrawn eccentric, so I was surprised to meet him easily at a social function here on Homeworld. The affair was a fundraiser supporting the Society for an Independent Annulus, and since that habitat resulted from the third Airafane Clip, which Ranglen found, maybe his being there was not unexpected.

I saw him standing on a balcony, alone, surveying the crowd. He looked relaxed, content with his isolated if vigilant perch (it had a good view). There was something appealing—even Romantic—about his chosen overlook and separate regard. It was commanding and yet private, "taking things in" while remaining withdrawn. Like a spy.

On a self-dare (I had read his publications and thought of him as a personal "hero"), I walked up to where he stood and talked openly. And I was shocked to find him easy to relate to.

He gave me his name without my requesting it, and then we spoke casually about the crowd below, his latest writings, the lecture career he since had abandoned, his fears of Annulus becoming over-developed. Though none of it was unique or surprising, he conveyed an earnestness I found appealing. His relaxed but not informal dress, his slimness, his craggy face, his wayward hair, his handsome if almost boyish features, and especially his eyes, coldly blue and more like stones than warm invitations—all made him "interesting," a person more given to irony than banter. I caught other people glancing at him too. And though he maintained an emotional distance, he was not impolite.

I still asked nothing about his private life, assuming he wanted no personal questions. But, since I *am* a publisher, I couldn't let this lucky moment pass. I asked, offhand, if he had any manuscripts he might need a home for.

He smiled, or maybe laughed. "Well, since you mention it…"

And I wondered then if our meeting was not accidental at all.

He pulled from his dress-jacket a ragged notebook, which he handed me with seeming trust.

It was filled with hand-written poems. He called them scribblings, accumulated over years, raw material not fully worked, more like exercises to keep his mind sharp. He doubted he'd ever come back to any of them. So he said, if I was interested, he'd consider their publication.

He warned me they wouldn't be what his more scholarly readers expected, but he assured me they were "completed enough" and not just notes.

I was overwhelmed but a little suspicious. Was there something too unique—or even disreputable—about these works that did not make them part of his standard oeuvre? And why surrender them now? Why to me and not his standard publishers? He seemed to be discarding, or "unloading," the book, like a real spy passing on dangerous secrets.

And he said that if I accepted it, all discussion about payment and editing would be done through his agent, that he himself would not review the final copy and would not be available for last-minute edits.

I must have shown my doubts despite my eagerness. So maybe to convince me, he insisted he was proud of the collection, but that he needed to "let it go," that it reminded him too much of events and places he wanted to forget—or that he no longer could remember, so reading the text bothered him. He said he normally wrote for specific audiences, but these poems had been written for himself, and out of a necessity he "no longer understood." He didn't need them now, he added, and so he was eager to "set them free."

He looked sad when he said this, almost like a parent abandoning a child.

And then, suddenly, he walked away. So quickly I couldn't stop him before losing him in the crowd.

I never saw him again.

And apparently no one else has. Soon after our meeting he vanished from Homeworld.

On a loose sheet inside the notebook I found contact information for his agent (not his usual agent, by the way). All arrangements, contracts, approvals and edits, were made through her. I was instructed to donate all author's royalties to the Society for an Independent Annulus, and that these donations should be acknowledged as contributions from my company alone. I also was given permission by the agent to disclose that information here.

The poems before you, then, except for minor corrections of spelling or uncertain hand-writing (many had been marked-up or revised), are exactly the way they appeared in the notebook. The collection's title and its organization came from a "table of contents" included at the end of the book, clearly a late addition.

The poems apparently were written after the third Clip had been discovered and while Annulus was being built, possibly including the time when the fifth Clip was found. I say this based on internal evidence, which is very shaky.

The works contain many contradictions, problems of timing, even of identity, as if written by a host of authors across eras. Clearly Ranglen uses as many disguises and masks in his works as he does in his life. During the editing I occasionally felt he was playing with me, that he *wanted* his reader to be a little baffled, or that the poems really were meant for only himself, and thus might be his version of insiders' jokes.

Or maybe—and this notion bothers me—the joke was not being played *by* him, but *on* him, by an enigmatic and "suspect" universe he was trying to understand.

Anyway, I present to you the contents of "the notebook" as it was given to me, with its assigned title, structure, and sub-headings, exactly as Mykol Ranglen wanted them. I added no footnotes, since I have no authority to write them. My own speculation is no more valid than any other reader's.

But be aware—or "beware"—the works here are inconclusive. They *tease*. They absorb as much light as they shed.

Which, given our troubled and contrary times, is maybe appropriate.

I hope you enjoy them.

Sites passed,
Travelers' ways,
Temporary planets for transitory days.

I. Nights on Alchera

The Branch Line Stop

Planet of Dreams,
Realm of magic,
Boreal setting
And cradle of desire,
One-time hope
For a singular future.

Now you are lost,
Found and gone,
To return in only
The small dreams of night,
Sought, probed,
In random excavations.

My world, *her* world:
Its haunted radiance,
Manifest nightmares,
Fleeting attractions,
Deep stellar secrets
And moments of awe.

But I can't come again.
Though a universe repeats,
It never retreats.
Even pale boundaries
And old laws persist.
I can make only temperate,
If extended, goodbyes.

In Another Country

In the old Dreamtime,
When the world was unformed,
The Sky Heroes walked
The fluid first lands,
And their footprints, bodies,
Wanderings and cries,
Gave shape to the finally
Stone-hard earth.

So walk with me then
On that path made by Heroes—
This hill once a thigh-bone,
That pool a fallen tear—
And discover their secrets
Writ on Dreamcave walls
In handprints, petroglyphs,
Opals, starred signs,
Think about our future,
See our lives in cryptograms,
Visit Maggie Springs
And walk-about our way,
With Carpet-Snake woman
And Sleepy-lizard man,
Spin our own Dreamtales,
Become wanderers new
In landscapes old—
Archetypes, but free.

So come on, Space Ranger,
It's time for us on earth,
Time to learn that love given
Is more than love achieved,
Time to walk upon world-lines
In settings of Dreams,
Time to think, time for two,
Where you'll play the game of me,
And I the game of you,
Time to find what we were,
What we are, and hope to be:
Maggie Springs,
The well, the water,
And thee.

The Heart Does Not Ask

Come to me entirely,
Come to me free.
Be equal, my likeness,
Find self in what you see.
End faith, end searching,
Entreat me, as I yield.
Let me hold you, let me love you,
Make solace, be fulfilled.
Like sculptors we'll touch,
Our minds will caress,
We'll be memory, pride,
Made of one true holiness.

So come to me resolved,
Come to me like waves
That annihilate the shore,
Come to me like fire
Or lightning on the sea.
And glide, submerge,
Lose boundary, station,
Space—lose hold!—
Abandon your aloneness,
And find yourself,
In me.

(for Mylia)

Cannibal at the North End of the World

Its face is green,
With white teeth and plum lips
Encircled by red.

Its helpers are three supernatural birds:
    Raven,
Who plucks out eyes and swallows them;
    Hokhokw,
Who cracks open skulls and eats brains;
    Crooked Beak,
Who kills with sudden sledgehammer blows.

The creature in its cold northern remove
Is both worshipped and feared,
And some say its voice contains secrets, philosophy,
Words out of time, prophecies in code,
Revelations of after-lives and means to all ends,
Challenges to eager unfed minds.

But, if you think on it, you soon know better.
Bottomless rapacity gives nothing back.
Its echoes are empty, its henchmen only brutes,
It's more maddened monster than restorative myth.
Its food is human life, that's all,
A singular appetite hardly profound.
And though some still hear from it
Insight and lore,
We know
What it really says:

"More!"

"More!"

Stations of the Light

Mr. Lonely, in his lighthouse,
Sent out signals every night.
But the ships, uncomprehending,
Sailed on, out of touch,
But *not* out of sight.

Lights in towers
Rise above the shore.
A beacon stops, a beacon starts.
Sure in one such Queen of Diamonds
Must reside my Queen of Hearts.

You say it is dangerous
To watch the moon in solitude.
But if I, when distant,
Gaze at it too, do I not then
Watch it with you?

To win a lone writer
Takes little work, and no fee.
All you need to say is,
"Make love to me,
In poetry."

On love I would write
If only this were true:
There be only one reader.
And that reader,
Only you.

When we touch, words fail.
We consume in desire.
Was it you,
Or I, then,
Who was born in fire?

Lighthouses at night
Are reliant and serene.
Keepers watch, ships sail.
The stars look down and conclude,
All is well.

Ice People

I'm wary and afraid
Of too much amazement,
Of saturating and deadening
My capacity for hope,
Of allowing my dreams
To leave me behind.

I watch new creatures
Emerge from glaciers
While huge shard blocks
Calve down into waves,
Collapsing apartments
Of urban ice renewal,
The convulsive splash
Sending frenzied birds
After churned-up fish,
As blue arenas gape open
In the white and ochre
Ice walls above.

And there, figures—unreal!—walk,
Alert, faceted, polished, hard,
With torsos blue and shoulders white,
With bodies scintillating deep within.
They step forth gaudily, newborn, stiff,
Animated icebergs in soft lowered light,
Fresh new yields of planetary enchantment,
Of intervention evolution given over to fancy,
Of astonishing lives in locked vault lands,
Embodied ice forms, frigid dynamics,
That haunt this world's spectral crown.

My mind reels—
I feel rampant emotions,
See reminders of climates
Long dead and departed,
Fastenings of winter,

Exterminating icicles
Searching for warm blood
(Or fleeing small flames),
Animation imitations,
Angels of glass,
Ancient deep chills
That want to lure,
Please, promise,
And finally break.

In tinkling glissandos
They tread near me,
Make distant chimes
Now lost to the world,
Retreating from the lack
Of distant human interest.

I wave to a Crystal Man.
But his eyes, black ice,
Stab back at my assumptions,
Critical, disheartened,
Wintry, cold.

Whatever could I say
To a diamond, anyway?

Asleep In the Arms of the Dragon

While you sleep,
Above you in the clear night sky,
The constellation Draco (the dragon)
Coils its jeweled, tentacular length,
Like a snake!—
In black-walled, white-gemmed caves.
Its eyes (two stars) like the North Star
Never set, and thus, they stare,
At your quiet, fitful, preoccupied ease.

But know that in legend the dragon
Stood for chaos, primeval flux,
The undefined, un-zero, prelude to order,
Before the coming of reasoning gods
And their later flawed independent creations.

Therefore, remember, as you prosper and build,
Put names to offspring, toy with ethics,
Demarcate time and organize space,
That, as you sleep, you also *dream*—
And you swim in the ancient miasma sea,
You are watched, and touched,
By this antique diminished primordial Satan,
This original demon of power, insane,
Now banished, retired, compromised, weak,
But still a haunt in your long sleep
That hints of disorder, fall, heat death,
Big Crunch, Big Dark, bottomless Long Night.

But…worry not,
Be reminded, nothing more,
That dreams are timeless:
They take you back, and forward,
To when the spiral-heaving dragon
Ruled in whirlpools, anti-clockwise cyclones,
And that now it only arches above you,
Serene, near a comfort, even reassuring

That we are not always, solely,
Ourselves.

So, be at peace.
Rest. You are weary.
And look toward tomorrow
With expectation and hope.
And feel no lurking
Suspense or peril
When you say
(In a whisper,
Of course),

"Yes,
All is well."

The Lighthouse Keeper

Each night, from the deep,
From beneath wet shrouds
And undefined dimensions,
Upheavals arise and are caught
In the interrogating clarity
Of my light.

Galleons of weed-encrusted wood
Peopled with pale-lit screaming ghosts,
Dinosaurs grappling with intestine-like squid
Amid shooting beads of luminescent foam,
Drowned spaceships tossing on their sides
As planets emerge, cities crash,
Moons take to the sky or swim,
Witch-fires lace the flotsam boil
And shine through eyes of corpse-gaunt pirates.
Whole universes spring into existence
Like quantum fluctuations
Between consciousness and death.

And I, aghast, full of wonder and fear,
Conductor and host of these primeval forms—
Tender of the night, keeper of the flame—
Feel my heart shake and my intellect freeze.

And I ask—are they mine?
Do I make and embellish
Or simply reflect?
Do these nightly visitations
Beckon and frighten
Yet know not of me?
Are they real, but separate?
Or my own, and not real?

Unable to answer,
I stare through the night,
Wrestling with secrets

In the crests and swells,
Pondering, excited,
Terrified, torn,
Seeking revelation
But longing to flee.

And I think,
"Solipsistic,"
Yet always suggestive,
Are the things

I see.

Barinda's Tale

The arc, the colored bow,
The frame around the Spider,
The crocodile serpent
That eats orphans who cry,
The spectrum river
That fell from the stars
To sew the landscape
And strangle marauders,
The Moyocks out of time.
It loved us, it saved us,
More than any fugitive
Self-satisfied Earth hero.

Its longing persists,
It wants back the life
We foolishly stole,
That once was bestowed
But not freely given,
That came from the sky
And the water and the earth,
And now, ambiguous,
Uninvited, from the night.

It wants us back.
It appraises the landscape
To call figures from the dark.
It builds its caverns
From earth-holes of isolation.
It's a snake with horns
That negotiates for victims,
That rattles its dangers
To control new lives.
It lurks and hovers.
It's a demon in a mountain,
In a crater, in the night.

We fought it in the past

But we lost to resurrections.
It fooled us with promises
And worldly benedictions,
With visions of lovers
Who returned too empty,
Who spoke and desired
But betrayed severed hearts.
Its colors are deceptive,
It's made of poison and blood,
Its illuminated forest
Probes us with mystery.
We have no past
To retaliate against.
We have just the Spider
And his prison, the Web,
Only the stranger
Who laid forth Time
And outsider Space,
His own hard ends
And sullen deep deaths.

Our bright creation
Redesigns itself,
Here, our planet,
Our cherished round Blight,
Where Airafane walked
And Moyocks prowled,
Where mighty were the fallen,
Where legacy cities
No longer stand.
But the Dreams continue.
We bury our dead
At cemetery crossroads,
At stations and ports
Where new lives depart.
We are planted, used,
Shaped—we evolve,
We live a Story
Whose unreliable voice
Tells poor secrets

To the vain and uninvited.

Remember that we owe,
Remember how landscape
Defines our choices,
That we're a foundation
Which needs to be vigilant,
That our Story has no end,
That it now draws heavy
To undefined obstacles
That, most likely,
Will not be ours.
So live with me, my people,
My Alcherans, my daughters,
Be one, be unleashed.
Make your own definitions
And write tales of grandeur.
Follow me, overtake me,
Leave me behind.
You have no need of me.
You are creation.

As It Fell

At night, in the snow,
By her powered-down,
Dim-lit aircar,
She stands.
Collar up, lips calm.
And she stares
Into the fragments
Of a peeling sky,
White condensation
From a ceiling black.

And she thinks,
Does the universe reach down to her?
Stare at her in wonder as she looks back in awe?
Can she find only visions of galactic indifference,
Or gift-chandeliers for our sole illumination?
Are the glints in her eyes only reflections
(Like fallen stars in tiny human seas),
Or signals of a higher intellect's grace?
Does the vast dark find her pensive look
As haunting as I, for instance, do?
Does it know a similar tender ache
When the snowdrops pool in globules on her lips?
On the moist, ripe, crescents of her lips?
Is longing interstellar? Is she loved by the sky,
As she is loved by me?

Ah, I don't know.
I just watch her, in the snow.
And I alone get to notice
That the flakes falling there
Make white constellations

In her midnight hair.

Manifest Station

I saw tentacles,
You saw serpents.
I encountered One Death,
You Seven Lights.
You always saw perfectly,
While I obscurely.

On panes of mist
I looked with your eyes.
You became me,
Though more logically
I was meant
To be you.

The wolf claiming power
Was a Moyock in disguise,
Or another Fool Dancer.
It's a lesson we learned
And, most likely,
Will have to learn again.

We wanted our home
Between the forest and the sea,
Between underworld and skyworld,
Between life and death.
And we almost had it there,
For a moment.

Changing Woman
Was nature and mystery,
Reproduction and birth.
White Skull Woman
Represented water.
But they're both unlikely.
They, of course, were not you.

Sand Paintings are made
From white gypsum,
Red sandstone,
Blue chrysocolla,
Yellow ochre and black charcoal.
A land of melting rainbows indeed.
And if left unattended,
The patterns soon resemble
The hot-spring crusts
On the floor of the Blight.

The rain people
Ride in their clouds.
Holy people march
As black and yellow males
Or blue and white females.
It almost made sense to us,
There, for a moment.

But at last came forgetfulness.
The details disappeared.
Then the voices,
Then the actions,
And then,
Only silence.

You,
And me,
And the planet.

Only silence.

You Are Not Of Them

"You are not of them,"
Said the gods to the child.
But since, in her folly,
She created those gods,
An all self-devouring
Perverse tautology,
A serpent with a belly
Devouring its own tail,
Rolls a fated,
Implacable wheel
At me, at you,
At everyone,
Alas.

And so, instead,
Let's imagine me
Saying this to you,
At the final closing-out
And fire-sale of the world.
As rose gardens crumble,
Mythologies dissolve,
And the universe blinks out
In final dissipation,
I'll try once more
To eternalize my love
And declare,
"You're not of them!"

Though springs
Lose their grip,
Clocks halt,
And darkness replaces
Electro-magnetism,
You still will live on,
The ideal after closure,
The rare perfect union
Of what you are

And what I see.

But since, like any god,
I created *that* you out of *this* you,
And since, in the end,
The ontology of tautology
Might be all we'll ever see,
I'll wish, as we're sundered,
I was *your* figment made,
Out of love, out of need,
That what you saw
Is what you wished.

And that, at world's end,
It was *you*
Creating me.

II. Rocket Punk

Notes Toward a Supreme Science Fiction

Thoughts experimental,
Speculations extreme,
Extrapolated futures
To galaxies
Serene.

Technological epiphanies,
Catastrophic lost times,
Unruly civilizations,
Or post-human
Sublimes.

Unrestricted subjects,
Dream-planets made real,
Designers filling emptiness
With constructions
Surreal.

Such far projected fictions
Are longings come true,
For worlds, wonders,
And a universe
Made of you.

But three subjects only
Can make *my* SF supreme:
The obsessed, the pursued,
And the space
In between.

Negotiating a Dream

How do you take
A future from the past
And reconstruct it
For the present day?

How do you distill
Its buried promise,
Purify its faults,
Keep its one-time
Social appeal
Of critiques shot
From under the table,
Its free and illicit
Pulp pleasures,
Its shared, exclusive
Sharp-spoken tongue?

How do you accept
Its alternate reality
That long since
Has been rendered unreal,
A foreign era's
Quaint projections,
Preserve the fragile naïveté
That once made an engine's
Call to action?

How do you acknowledge
Whims as serious?
Keep those future
Flights of fiction
From becoming today's
Harmless fantasy?
Maintain their once
Ready scenarios
As yet still suitable
Post-future worlds?

Reclaim what's best
From a time archaic,
A period out of touch,
Even vaguely obscene?

How do you translate
Their star-touched hope
Into applied
Objective correlatives,
Goals for the *not*-so-inexperienced,
And less-than-cosmic
Patrons of today?

Is a dead society's
Order required?
Are dreams locked
To their spawning roots?
Must looking ahead
Be always grounded
In a mired past?

With newfound Clips
Came new space regimes.
So, can we negotiate,
Maybe even appropriate,
Some other era's
Lost stellar dreams?

The Secrets of Earth

"Where do they hide them?"
The space marauders say,
Looking down with tentacle-encircled eyes
Onto the beckoning blue nugget of Earth.
"In what basins, what caves,
Are the ancient treasures hid?
The weapons, the baubles, the spoils,
The loot?"

But oh, how disappointed they'd be,
If they heard, as a woman once told me,
In my search for romance and secret depth,
That, she shrugged, and said she had little,
That "What you see is what you get."

The Earth's no vault of hidden plunder,
No front, no veil, no prehistoric cache.
Trinkets aren't hidden in cold mountain caves
Or buried in chambers beneath the sea.
Even our huge diverse old world,
With all its splendor, experience, and age,
Has no hidden ruins, no ancient gods,
No races lost in cities under ice.
It has only *people*,
And more of those each day,
Clouded water, smoked air,
And heaps of rampant life,
In debt.

So,
"Sorry, guys."
To all space raiders,
Desperados, and thieves,
We have little to hide
And too much to regret.
In the end,
You needn't bother.

What you see
Is what you get.

Loving the Spaceport

A multifaceted electric power plant;
A railroad yard with rockets on end;
A Cape Canaveral spacious and broad;
A sinister labyrinth infested with spies.

These are my four getaway realms,
My harbors to elsewhere, providers of escape.
Maybe they lead to only more confinement,
But—who cares? Nothing matters on departure.
These are my *spaceports!*

They are places where Earth and sky meet,
Where sutures untie and clamps lift,
Where cranes, towers, ramps, pylons,
Conduits, bus bars, breakers, condensers,
Fill some retro power-plant switchyard
Designed by a mad Tesla or Piranesi,
Where faux step-up transformers act
As spastic "blast-off synchronizers" in heat,
Their hard bouquets of high-voltage bushings
Whining countdowns for tense ignitions,
For explosively dramatic flame-bowl lift-offs,
As if frenzied electromagnetic induction
Can kick-start a spaceship's jump from Earth.
Silver ogun needle-tipped rockets
Poise on flawless aesthetic curved fins,
Set and ready for their leaps into space.
Highly-charged metallic hums saturate
Transmission lines, cooling vanes, radiators,
Stepped-up voltages that boost rockets
Into a wide ozone heaven fraught
With tyrants, renegades, suzerains of evil,
Wayward comets and jostling moons,
All the skulking dangers of space,
Managed by square-jawed intrepid agents
Of United Earths and Off-World Planets.

Or, it's like a railroad shuffling yard,

A maze of interlaced steel tracks
With wooden enclosed observation towers,
In which the levers are primitive and big,
Where the spaceships are moved on rugged flatcars
By tough little steam-run switching engines,
Where missiles rest on hydraulic cradles
That raise them to angled or vertical positions,
Readied for explosive rapid-fire launch,
To be shot off like warheads puncturing the sky.
All iron mainlines lead to outer space,
To the standing rockets that share the yard
With dispatchers, consists, empties, stations,
Intricate bridges and racks of signals,
Whose colored filters under blackened hoods
Flash their secret messages in code,
Where semaphore towers swing colored arms
As if sending reassuring but hurried goodbyes.
Struts lift the launchers into place,
Vast arks sit like upturned whales,
To carry migrants, refugees, orphans,
Escapees from old repressive governments
To the lush freedoms of the outer planets,
This anachronistic near World War scene
Allowing rebels from snowbound hideaways
To gather and warm in clouds of steam,
Where railroads end and space begins,
Where they leave their cloying pasts behind
And uplift, depart, and rocket away.

Or, in sunlit spaces beside big oceans,
On a vast sea-grass open plain,
Densely detailed red-and-white gantries
Stand by concrete pads for brute-like boosters
With tiny insignificant payloads on top,
Small winged vehicles on towers of bombs
Filled with highly inflammable fuels,
Tetrazine, hydrazine, good-old kerosene,
The sides frigid with ice and vapors,
To make monstrous pillars of flame exhausts,
Blasting longer than the spaceships themselves,

Leaving charred the yellow launch cradles
Like seared metal racks blackened in ovens,
Where Vehicle Assembly Buildings
Hold abstract and self-contained worlds
Layered with decks and efficiency lights,
Where at night the poised white leviathans
Stand flood-lit like dangerous experiments,
Extravagant, politicized, controversial, debated,
Where the moods of workers almost grow sterile,
Too vigilant, rational, engineered, joyless,
The costs too high, the politics too classified,
The bureaucracy too blanketing and grim—
But it all goes away at the moment of detonation,
When crowds go wild, turn into children,
Cheer, laugh, shout, high-five,
As the huge expensive angelic monster
Plows on its glaring inferno—into the sky.

Or, it's a noir subterranean city at night,
Where villains prowl on strange tasks,
Where victims are caught in blast-off flames,
Where lovers, spies, smugglers meet
In this legally illuminated yet many-shadowed
Factory at night, with its murky freighters
Hiding illegal and top-secret cargos,
Where crooks, thugs, outlaws, thieves
Live in a dark underside of futurism,
Where Cape Canaveral becomes Cape Fear,
Where the beaconed spaceport is like Naked City,
Where men in fedoras and tight trench coats,
Where women in heels, furs, slanted hats
Slink up gangways to dark tramp freighters,
In compromised exits and desperate moves
(Your rocket leaves where the slidewalk ends),
Saying farewell to all their lovelies, their bad secrets,
Their broken dreams and brittle hard pasts,
Their short love-ties and their long goodbyes,
Their set-ups, pit-falls, panics and shocks,
Their recurring year zero, their last ground zero,
Which make even this place of free departure

Yet one more labyrinth deception,
Where suddenly pulled-up getaway ladders
Make Berlin Walls for all anxious fugitives,
Caught in spotlights, retaken, repossessed,
Right at their moment of pinnacle flight.

These are the places where we all seek lift-off,
Wait for the crane to wheel itself back,
For the flames to lick at the curved fins
And for spaceships to rise on yet more impressive
FX propulsions, channeled dynamite,
To fly into gossamer cirrus skies
And reach promised worlds of quartz and jade.

We are rocket punks, we are travel crazy,
We live by night and drive point blank
From lonely places to scarier worlds,
To bask beneath lightning-cracked skies,
Whose patterns of archaic television interference
Hover and glide in electric nights.

But we still want to go,
Kiss the past goodbye,
Get launched from spaceports
Just like these
And reach the mute stars
That beckon above.

Always, we want to go....

Up-up,
And away.

Crystal, Fire, Rainbows, and Light

You'll find me at the base
Of Jewel Mountain on Krypton,
By its platinum orogeny of set cut gems,
Or its Fire Falls, its Rainbow Canyon,
Its Gold Volcano or Scarlet Jungle—
Its crystal, fire, rainbows, and light.

Even Little Redemption had Crystal Pillars,
Faceted fingers with empty mirrors,
Blue-white, pink, and yellow glass spikes,
Expiations of guilt in the grim Sunken Plains.
Even Alchera, from what I remember,
Sported its own crystal soldiers, flame folk,
Multicolored and parti-textured growth.

Planets too are like colored gems,
Like hanging jewels on velvet space,
Signal radiants for a secular divine.
They match the four qualities of gemstones:
Hardness, durability, rareness, beauty.
Though gems are too solid to be supernatural,
They yet are *more* than natural instead—
Intensifications, distillations of nature,
Spiritual lights in an empty dark,
Their fractal reflections like tiny space-warps,
Small breeders of living fire, colors pure,
Exotically shaped sensory splendors,
Tightly wound spaces, trinkets like thrones.

And planets also are like Deep Time
Captured in brilliant, polished containers,
Wells for the inhuman souls of the universe,
Globes of stained glass in black cathedrals,
Where a high Gothic saturated light
Makes fascinating, even dangerous, colors,
A "light through" instead of "light on,"
Intrinsic, inborn, echoing, profound,

Where pigments shout in primary shades,
Where sensory cognition is teased and unbalanced:
Red-desert dunes under bright pink skies,
Yellow-green heavens above dark-green grass,
Violet-blue trees under golden-yellow clouds,
Rocks splashed with carmine and orange
While green rabbits run on peach sands.
I feel we *all* live in alien worlds now,
And that every description is like a first contact,
Making planets into jewels
From the mines of dark matter,
The wealth of the universe,
The opals, prisms, beacons, and eyes.

When we search for wonders
On the backdrop of night,
We prefer the essentials:
Crystal, fire, rainbows, and light.

What Flash Gordon Said to Dale Arden

Well, here we are, ourselves again.
I feel we're at the end of some pop-culture history.
You were "girl Friday," then feminist, independent.
I was era chauvinist, then rediscovered sensitive.
They labeled you "jealous" and I "brute hero"—
Tags hardly complex—but at least we escaped
The latter and nasty "bitches and wimps."

And now we've achieved this tentative equilibrium.
You, businesswoman, build spaceships now.
You're nurturer of policy, wealth, power.
And I fly those ships, test them and tame them,
Still your mellowed-out maturing boy,
Still drawn by adventure, outer space, and you.

We'll meet some night in one of your ships,
Alone in a landing field emptied by winter.
Outside, the snow will settle around us
And rise in pillows by the sleek metal fins.
I'll wear my fur-lined jacket with scarf,
You in long coat, pony-tail, and boots.
We'll look like models of a special pulp era,
Or elegant lovers from the nuclear age,
When deserts were atomic, watches glowed,
Clocks resembled atoms and airports were malls,
When UFOs stalked with post-war paranoia,
When telescopes on mountains nudged the stars,
And walking into the woods at night
Could lead to a dangerous alien encounter.

We'll sit quietly in the spaceship lounge,
Lit by colored instrument lights,
And talk of all we encountered in space,
The adventures, thrills, fabulous escapes,
Not saying much we haven't said already.
We've been part of each other too long now
To surprise ourselves with new revelations,

Our words not meant to enlighten any more,
But to draw us closer to each other's regard,
In a mildly intimate well of gravity.

And I'll remind you, express my delight,
Of how you became the compatriot,
Partner, equal explorer, and rogue, in my life.
You were never plaything or "stewardess" to me.
You were perfect *because* you were real.
Only the critics wanted to change us,
Make me into crude Teutonic stallion
And you overwrought resentful toy-girl
(Imitating their own unrecognized brutalities).
They said I loved quests and that you loved me,
But I only wanted excitements that I shared with you.
They colored our pleasures as weak and naïve,
As kept between the panels (even in the "gutters"),
But they were crass fools to cheapen our love,
Our great impassioned Old Earth's longing.

Still, even now, in our newly settled romance,
I can't help questioning why you loved me.
I was more sensitive to oppressed workers,
And those not even recognizably human,
Than I was to feisty, sharp-eyed you.
But I missed you so much when you weren't with me.
I'd have taken you always if the "creators" allowed it.
Besides, you stowawayed often enough—
Much to my chagrin, and much to my joy.
I was so impressed by your tenacity, devotion.
And I never saw it as devotion to *me*—
I was the unthinking if sturdy male idol,
So clumsily out of touch that I thought
You came for the same reasons I did:
The cause, the mission, the obsession to do good.
I was too preoccupied with saving worlds,
Too stereotype "champion" to see that your incentive
Might be more personal, tender, and warm,
More *human*, than my unsubtle conditioned reflex.
You were jealous, true, but I secretly adored that,

And you weren't jealous of what I really wanted anyway—
Adventure, mystery, new skies and planets,
The stars grouped in foreign constellations,
And seeing them, I realize only now, with you.

After leading rebellions against tyrant Ming,
Our sights rose to new cosmic spaces.
Social eras passed. Politics changed.
But why did we have to let *their* futures take us?
We did so much before *Star Trek* platitudes
Cut and bandaged lost causes of awe,
Before Clips entangled all futures with knots,
Redesigned destiny and crumbled our rockets.
Why did we have to upgrade to *their* bleak standards?
Why can't we exploit our own long love?
What's wrong with our humble retrograde selves?
Yes, I know that one day I'll lie broken,
Left to die after all spaceships crash,
When, at last, I'll have to pay for my dominion,
My callow, man-boy, hollow self-interests—
Poisoned on a death-world, coagulating my life—
Where, I assure you, as I finally pass on,
I'll think only of my time…with you.

So, for now, if just for this moment,
I'm glad for the heavy darkness outside,
For tonight's isolation, for this private peace.
The gathering snow is our ally tonight.
I soon must leave on another long mission,
Abandon you to economics you now handle so well.
You always were the designated adult,
And I the simple if strapping clown.

And I know what will happen
When I'm out there in space,
Alone in darkness, scanning the controls,
Seeking small failures and hairline faults,
Where, suddenly, I'll hear a small sound,
A whisper, a rustle, a soft interruption,
And I'll remember, sadly, in my sensual vacuum,

Your quiet moves as you paced on board,
That shadowy walk, that gliding turn,
That long-skirted murmur behind me,
Your attention, your affection…

And then,
Full of happy expectation,
I'll turn to see you—
And I'll find…
Nothing.
Just the empty cabin,
Its aloneness, desolation,
And my old tired self
When it's without you.

Yet, with a pure and lovely
Science-fictional irony,
I'll recollect as I'm there,
That your eyes
Are blue of Earth,
And black of space
Is your hair.

Litanies of Worlds

Jungle planets where tree-trunks sing,
Egg moons in nests of debris,
Worlds with targets, octopi clouds,
Globes with hoops or internal dynamos,
Colored candies, Life Savers, Charms,
Wheels of planets in necklace beads,
Orbs alive, rhomboid, square,
With rocks that leer or flowers that dance,
With searchlight fish and fruit-like eyes,
Where violet gazelles under lemon skies
Chase fugitive owls of soft lime-green.

Will we find ourselves
On these bright new planets,
Discover abundance, wealth, delight?
Will we again become youngsters
Sporting in arenas of stellar success?
Will we play with toys strangely profound,
Crunch new identities from alien strata,
Probe exotic continental shelves
And roam in lofty air-streams free?

Or maybe we'll become just petty hoarders,
Latter-day Brainiacs, stealing cities
Squeezed into bottles for private display.
Collecting, after all, exhibits power.
But it's sensory too, like old Uncle Scrooge
Kissing his money, swimming through coins
In a fine exuberance of fluid self,
Where objects are subjects,
And we finally become what we behold,
Ourselves absorbed in our own accumulation.

Will we stockpile landscapes?
Package planets, or set them in stands?
Enter them in contests to win over admirers,
Brag about chalcedony or lapis worlds,

Jupiters like agates, jaspers like Mars,
The snowflake obsidian of Pluto's surface,
The aquamarine of the clouds of Uranus?
Will we hide capitalism, ideology, hegemony,
Inside the colors and cuts and angles
Of sapphire stars—cobalt, canary, delicate blush—
In constellations of iridescent jewels
For black and satin sterling-glass trays?

Will we caress, or will we possess?
Show off what we hold, or only touch?
Preserve our delicate fine new planets,
Or mount them, like glowing stones of power
In selfish rings for private delectation?
Or will we, more crude, just store them in vaults?
Will Clip-liberation lead to only
More forms of insidious control?

When the galaxy's ornaments
Fall into our hands,
Which of two reactions
Might claim our favor?

Will we consume?
Or will we savor?

Touching the Night Sky

The sky was closer then,
Soon to be reached
By a new space program's
Ascendant technology.
Budding astronauts
Seemed like juveniles,
Felt they could flee
Gentle Earth's cradle,
Join an adult cosmic sky,
Have their mettle, manners,
And knowledge tested
By respectfully accepting
Alien outsiders,
Meet the universe
And then become heroes,
Saviors of days.

They watched the stars
From night-lit patios,
Or kindly graded nearby hills,
Scoped their new
Celestial neighbors
Who, even then,
Were a bit too ominous.

The Earthlings knew if *they*
Could touch their own night sky,
Then it, in turn,
Could reach down to them—
With grappling hooks
From raiding flying-saucers,
Or large hands
Stretching over the horizon,
Depositing captives
In cloaked mother-ships
That whisked them away

Behind iron curtains of space.

Open fields at night
Could become launchpads,
And the woods—all were closer
To the houses back then—
Hid downed spaceships
And derelicts in caves,
Canted half-buried saucers
Abandoned by stealth crews,
Who left to infiltrate innocent Earth.

Mysterious glows leaked from houses,
E.T.'s snuck into suburbs at night,
Aliens in disguise rode on subways
And spied for distant fortress planets
Spinning nearer in orbits of peril.
Castaway Martians walked the streets,
Avoided lampposts, pesky porch-lights,
Hid the pain and tears of their longing
As they waited for Mars finally to rise,
Distant, beckoning, as big as the Moon.
They cried, then schemed,
In order to get home.

Fear of "the other" kept people distressed.
They keenly scrutinized the skies above
For big Red missiles or little green men.
So many evenings found them staring
Through clear stratospheres into the universe,
At strident stars that pledged invasion,
Stellar imperialism, galactic supremacy.
Their obsession with empires filled heaven
And reflected back onto fresh ripe Earth.

Hilltop observatories
Doubled as guard-posts,
The first line of defense
Against interstellar attack.
Lonely telescopes aimed outward

Not to discover exotic science
But to see what evils
Grimly approached.
Mountain peaks were unsafe,
The first spots to be occupied
If cosmic war came to Earth.
Hovercraft hid in extinct volcanoes,
Cloud-camouflaged installations
Built weapons for nearing doomsday.
(The abominable snowmen were aliens, of course.)
The tallest hills and the deepest trenches
Hid far too many off-world secrets,
Lives not ours,
Bombs that ticked.

They believed, yet feared
An ideology of Evolution,
That life flourished in every pit and crack,
Came in diverse densities, degrees,
Lived in rocks, dunes of sand,
In clouds, flames, electricity, gas.
They worried, and wondered,
That creation didn't stop
After six legal days.

To this intense abundance of life
They responded with their own material excess.
They sent their consumerism
And product-mania even off-world—
Refrigerators to the stars, toasters on Titan,
Waffle-irons shaped like chromium aircars.
Middle-class gadgetry normalized space,
And free markets defeated stellar foes.

Conformity lay too heavy on the land,
Bred paranoia, insensitivity, fear.
They wanted—but dreaded—
Social connections to the Galactic Union.
Though curious, they lived frightened lives:
They might need to shake hands

With darkly-scaled and maybe slimy
Bare creature claws.
Latent prejudice powered both
Their arrogance and timidity.
To say they were conflicted
Was no laughing matter.

And yet…in the end,
Are *we* even good enough
Now to judge them?
They had nothing to work with
Except themselves,
No reference, no rubric.
They were pitifully poor
And untouched by the universe,
Until it suddenly fell onto them,
In a lifetime, in a moment.
They had just discovered
Atomic powers,
Keys to new kingdoms,
Rocket-engineered getaway illusions.
They looked into the future
Without our known filters of history.
They were still adolescents,
Struggling to enter
The purely unknown
And highly ambiguous
New worlds in space.
They had only what they had,
Which, to be honest,
Was not very much.

And did we become like them
When we discovered Clips,
Found our unique means of reaching,
If on borrowed technology,
Our own contemporary interstellar space?
Did we too manifest
These middle-class 20th-century fears?
Feel the same uncertainty

On whether we'd be good enough?
Was our new cosmic freedom also
Just a bit too strange, too big,
Too scary and unsure?
Will our current space ventures thus fail?
Our swelling economy weaken and die,
Drift into vague undefined disasters,
Grunge futures, cyberpunk wars,
Grimdark scenarios invading our zeitgeist,
Terrors of post-YA apocalypse?

Will we also look outward
Without seeing what's behind?
Are we running away so as not to be hurt?
Discarding dependents to keep ourselves free?
Becoming ultimately less to ourselves?

Is our politics any better?
Our well-wrought schemes any more liberated?
Will a fixed still-point come to our aid?
Will a Singularity Clip ever be found
With its coded galactic inclusive explanations?
Will new and cherished sought-after visions
Remain no bigger than our meager selves,
Give back nothing we don't have already?
So, what's to do?
Should we look to *them*, see as they saw?
Mine the past, think like a dinosaur?
Fly their streamlined muscle-car rockets
As well as our Clip-run utility RSV's?
Our poor precursors are too outdated,
Their ignorance is no longer justified,
Their lack of experience no excuse.
And we know so much more right now.

And yet, and yet,
They still dreamed,
They still *looked up*.

To all you ancient watchers of space,

You who observed with your innocent eyes,
Who briefly lived under imaginary stars
And thought science fiction
Could take you to the universe,
Answer your questions,
Prepare you the way...
Can you aid us, guide us?
Warn us of all our possible sins,
Define the dangers,
Clarify self-deceptions?

Will you help us to see,
Through your one-time
Bright and star-lit eyes,
How to touch, with integrity,
Our *own* night skies?

The Universe in a Frame

Tom Corbett, from the control deck
Of his Polaris spaceship, observed stars
Through a round window nearly his height
And cleverly encircled by pill-shapes of glass.

Rocky Jones with his visi-screened bulkhead
Made viewing the cosmos as easy
And controlled as flipping TV channels,
Once the negative image was reversed.

And in *The Forbidden Planet*,
A simulacrum of outer space
Came locked inside a plexiglass sphere
Sitting in the center of the pilot's round table,
Reproducing exteriors with small lights
And a tilted toy-like model of the ship.

Thus foreign majesty was often contained,
Restricted by limits rectangular or round.
Even their Cinemascope came in a letterbox,
And Panavision narrowed that width even more.
The great unbridled galactic surround
Was encountered in flat geometric screens.
It made a confining, a *domestic*, sublime.
They did see the universe, but only in a frame.

If the emotional goal of space travel is wonder—
Awe, reverence, surprise, transformation—
Then such imposition of Enlightenment margins
Could only hamper boundless sensations,
Restrict the majestic, clog the undefined.
How is one transported
Through tiny scratched windows?
Soar and seek "beyond the infinite"
In merely a few centimeters of screen?
How do you smash all comprehension,
Break free of the box, leap "one step beyond,"

When heads-up displays classify infinity,
And when just *seeing* vastness
Imposes immediate self-definition?

They surely craved more.
They had to have been like us.
They too must have asked
How one can astonish,
Break common sense,
Ruin suspension,
Affront comprehension,
And deliver grandeur
In something else than a cage?

We acknowledge the universe.
We catalogue and define.
We admire its beauty.

But we *want* the Sublime.

The October Crime

Not all stories
Involve spaceships.
This one's a murder
That takes place in autumn.

The novel lasts a month,
Parallels the season
From first color change
To last fallen leaf.

The setting's a small rural town
In southern N.Y. or northern Pa.
Low mountains and woods,
Mid 20th century.

A dead body's found,
A local young woman
On a dry crackling
Funeral bed of leaves.

She was the friend
Of a newly hired teacher
At a local high school,
Affectionate, not his lover.

The man reads science fiction.
He's rapturous about the future,
Its coming spaceflight, new technology,
The opening universe.

He teaches a class on SF.
He assigns an anthology
Covering the year, say, 2021.
He also tries to probe the murder.

Investigation, and recalling the woman,
Form the bulk of the story.

They give a portrait of the time and place,
The social, sexual, class milieu.

The police don't listen to him.
He's too new to the town.
He feels unaccepted and snubbed,
Like a marginalized SF alien.

He sees that the Native Americans
Who once inhabited the region,
The Seneca, the Iroquois,
Are treated the same.

He uses SF genre filters
To lightly critique
The assumptions of the town,
The privilege of its social, racial majority.

His search for a culprit soon stalls,
The leads become unproductive,
And autumn conducts its quiet
Decline in fire and ash.

(The *process* of autumn
Will be stressed through the story:
The daily changes and moody detail,
The exquisite decay.)

One night a colleague
Reads his SF anthology,
Says it's nonsense,
Inaccurate, a joke.

This man paints a dark *other* future,
Of terrorist chaos, media inundation,
Gender upheaval, racial violence,
Environmental collapse.

It's not the jet-pack wonder-world
Beloved by the teacher.

He's disappointed in the new technology
And shocked by the drastic social change.

In classic SF dialectical fashion,
He sees his own assumptions
Objectified, unfavorably assessed,
Framed in critical new perspectives.

"No fancy space travel,"
The other man claims,
"Just blow after blow,
New addictions to petty ideas.

Politics cheapened and based on lies,
Constant spiteful un-atomic wars,
Everyone clamoring for selfish rights,
Order lost, big shootings in crowds."

(The story's trick, of course,
Is that *today's* readers
Of the 22nd century will know
This history to be mostly true.

Enough references will be used,
Recognized if vague events,
To show the depiction is quite accurate,
Though rather slanted.)

"The real future," says the man,
"Is debased, decentered,
Its yields abundant but arbitrary,
Respect for *men,* like us, lost.

What you're feeling now—
This undercurrent of distress,
This encroaching bleak hysteria—
Will become the new social norm.

Your anthology's deluded,
Its rationalism a fraud,

Its stories blasé about all imminent
Racial, social, and sexual rage."

The protagonist is appalled,
His grand faith in upward
Spiraling Western progress
Trampled and shattered.

But the other man's scenario
Sounds *too* realistic,
Too clearly "argued,"
Too much an affront.

And he remembers the murder,
The slow decay of continual autumn,
And he wonders, suddenly—
How does the man *know*?

How can he relate so many
Grim "facts" of that time,
Depict it with such dark emotion,
Certainty, and caustic put-down?

He recalls a common
SF plot of his day:
Escapees from a "bad" future,
Hiding, disguised, in the present.

With this insight he declares,
"You and the woman are from the *future*.
She was an agent sent to retrieve you.
And you killed her—in order to hide here.

You want me to hate your contentious world,
To label its progress as just prejudice,
And though all you say about it is frightening,
It's *you* who can't take its change.

You came here to find a 'simpler' era,
A place you thought still supported

All your assumed 'natural' powers,
But you can't escape your *insecurity*.

You had to be archaic in your world,
Out of touch, a fossil, a relic,
And when a time-agent followed you here,
You quickly removed her, had her killed."

The other man only taunts in reply,
"But who would believe you?
Your SF might help *you* to understand.
But others from this time? Not a chance!"

And the teacher feels only despair.
Both his future *and* his present
Have now been condemned,
Uncovered by new cognitive estrangement.

He flees the man—he suspects,
Horribly, in personal shame,
That the traveler might reflect
His *own* era-fraught biases and fears.

He runs, leaves town,
Drives into Indian-haunted woods—
And encounters one more
Known SF scenario.

He can't escape,
All roads turn back.
He keeps driving forward
And yet he re-enters his own town.

He tries again. The road returns,
As if the village is self-contained,
A setting with no exits,
A location under glass.

Maybe the whole locale
Is false, a 50s façade,

A synthetic refuge, a resort
For intolerant out-of-time fugitives.

And maybe he too
Is just an actor, manufactured,
Filling the scripted role of "hero"
In a prearranged looping story.

He's caught now in landslides of doubt,
Suspicions of private and public worlds,
His classic ideal of objective analysis
Melting into pits of bottomless horror.

But the town lives on,
Adrift in its autumn,
In the recurring, if endless,
Season's alteration.

No wonder they picked autumn, he thinks.
Summer would be too static.
They needed an accepted *sense* of change,
A color-coded, if lying, wheel.

And no wonder they picked *him*,
The token voice of token reason,
So easily and profoundly exposed,
Destabilized, weakened, shot down.

And the murder too—
It must be part of the fable,
Must happen again, again, and again,
Both life, and leaves, in a constant fall.

The story thus shows the time's paranoia,
The *other* side of progressive SF,
The pesky disturbance that always lurks
In each self-liberating social observation.

He's inside his own fiction now,
He's become both figure and ground,

His world has been fully deconstructed
(Though he doesn't yet know that term).

And autumn too—
It's just another player,
A secret hooded elemental figure
Always shedding its many-colored skins.

The season's a model for cheap process,
For observers who don't want it to be real.
A histrionic cover, a masquerade,
Time's arrow made in jest.

How does the story end?
I sadly don't know.
I'm sure I'll never write it.
It lacks both destination—and brakes.

I have only this simple structure now,
This Möbius coil that's oddly entwined
With long corridors of leaking gold,
With mysteries, fade-outs, broken mists.

It's just a small SF tale
Within some bigger darker narrative,
Where the teacher's assumptions
Are repeatedly broken, rebuilt, destroyed.

And my red season of constant change,
In its simulated and stationary time,
Will go on to hide this ever recurring,
And ever sinister, October crime.

Adam Strange Returns to Alanna

Once more,
I await my grand departure,
Here in my select southern spot
With Centaurus above me,
Awaiting once more the zeta-beam
That will strike me, fling me,
25 trillion miles or more,
In a flash—

To you.

I do this not because I'm an adventurer,
A traveler of space, a scientist, a hero.
I don't come 4.3 light-years
To test my ingenuity and courage
Against monsters, menaces, disasters, villains.
I know the people of your world believe
I'm just some vain imperialist Lord
Who feels he alone has the right stuff
To save their precious, frightened planet.

But no, dear Alanna.
None of that matters.
I come only for you.

The green sky of your world is fascinating,
The open class system, the archaic city-states,
The advanced technology and wide free prairies
So full of new creatures, exploration, delight.
But none of that matters.
The only wonder that touches me is you.
I fight those villains not to be daring
But because they take me away from you:
The cruel Tornado-Tyrant, the mean Dust Devil,
The Crystal Conquerors and the Fadeaway Doom,
Even the Beast With the Sizzling Blue Eyes
(Which you, laughing, called me once).

I defeat them not because they threaten
But because they distract me away—
From you.

I come all this distance
And find every time some stupid monster
Eating the city or irradiating the landscape,
Turning people into water or smoke,
Mineral, fire, vapor, crystal—
And it's *lost time!* Lost—
Because my own personal "fadeaway doom"
I never can conquer.
In the pay-back of fate
It cheats me, every time.
How often, after the menace was defeated,
I'd take you in my arms,
Feel your warmth and softness against me,
Know the pleasure of touching you once more.
And then...
Nothing!
Betrayed again by that cursed zeta-beam
That gives so much,
And then takes so much away.
I fade,
And return to distant Earth,
Where I stand, very much as I stand right now,
Staring at bleak untouchable stars,
Around which, one of which,
You abide.

But no sorrow now.
I await departure and not return.
Soon I'll be with you!—
If all goes well, if you haven't been
Attacked, captured, kidnapped, killed!
Oh please, dear universe, let her be safe.
Let her stand there alive, awaiting me still,
Desiring me ever,
Eager once more for my instant arrival.

Come now, zeta-beam!

Drop me in her arms
And let me, please, have time this *time*
To show how much I love her.
Land me softly in a field of orange grass
Where I'll hold her, roll with her,
On cushioned ground under kind green skies,
Kiss her in the double-shadowed sunshine,
Feel life once more.

And I say—I declare!—
To all stars above,
You can keep your universe.
I want only her.
She is my landscape, my alien world,
My adventure and mystery and secret joy.
I know it can't last, but I accept that decree.
I'll remove what dangers might threaten her planet,
I'll pay my debt for this miracle deliverance.
But know—
I save her city because she lives there,
I rescue her world because it is *her* world.
You need never question my motivation
Because—believe me—
I do it all for her.

Ah! My countdown's started.
Seconds now! Soon!
Yes, zeta-beam, shower me with light,
With instant transfer to Far Centaurus.
6, 5, 4, 3,
Stars and distance—
Alanna!—
Take me.

First Light

When you first step onto an alien world…

You leave your soul behind,
Your brain uncouples like an unleashed drone,
Enthrallment creates sudden danger,
You feel dropped into shattered soft glass,
Colors grow and become unruly,
Lights spark from unknown interiors,
Details call for equal attention,
Old standards of perception dissolve,
Order tilts and is made vertiginous,
First encounters crowd and bully you,
Sights unfetter and distance flattens,
No barriers stop you from the *not*-you,
Forests illuminate and mountains grow eyes,
A razor-shrub shoots darts in your brain,
You stand on a crumbling human brink,
Input's a landslide, nothing's subordinate,
You're a newly-bought telescope
Now opened suddenly to *first light*—
And you drown in sensation,
You can't evade, explain,
You feel hard pressure,
You're sharpened and numbed,
You sense a creeping and brutal transformation,
Outlines blur, run like tears,
You're swept by a fierceness of sudden enchantment,
You're radically lost in destroyed definitions,
Your clarity melts, you exceed experience,
Your past and your future are broken and hurled…

When you first step onto an alien world.

III. Planetary Romance

After the Ball

It's no longer personal.
I now tremble not a bit.
But I know several times
When someone encountered
Turned worlds inside out,
Questioned resolve,
Tangled decision,
Confused direction,
Even led me to a plunge,
To cast all on a card,
Bet the house,
Take on destiny,
If only just to shatter
Quaint distinctions
And timid expectations.

But it's too far beyond
Discomfiture now.
Only allowed feelings
Persist.

So, there it is.

As I was,
At times.

The Lady In the Tramp

Yes, my child
Of half-eclipsed night,
Keep your selves distant
And never intermingle.
Wear satin in white
And velvet in shadow.
Be wild in contradiction,
Ambiguous, haunted,
And stay my white lily
In jet black leather.
Never balance,
Mix, join, or settle,
For opposites negate,
Extremes meet in
A muddled dull middle,
The resulting compound
Neutral and gray,
Diluted, limp.
And you'd fade,
Dark lady,
Fade like a memory,
Like yesterday's
Dim weather—
Oh yes, soft tramp,
Demon's angel
And sun's dark shade,
You'd fade,
Fade,
Fade…
All together.

The Assent

When she said yes…

My longing poised, hovered, took breath,
I felt washed in a pool of sudden accord
Between singular desire and ambiguous truth,
Adrift though still, alone yet near,
Swept clean of boundaries and filled with light,
Watched by a host as surprised as I
While the universe leaned across my shoulder
To find what miracle happened tonight.
Engines of want purred inside me:
I seemed a vessel for existence itself to shout,
"I exist! You dreamers should all believe in me more!"
The suddenly real made faith easy.
My eyes were like gifts, my hands special tools,
My smile a benediction
On all has-beens and all yet-to-bes,
On still-points, change, the surprises of time.
Gravity in tender cords flowed through me.
I heard sounds from Jupiter. My fingers grew trees.
Comets teased me and framed her with haloes.
She looked coy, eager, precious, alive.
Oh, I *was* the universe! It sang in my veins—
The skies, the stars!
I swear—
It was no less—

When she said yes.

In a Moment

You'll know them when they love you.

When they admit, as in a confessional,
When they declare, as in a court,
When they put themselves in danger,
When they write their surrender and sign their release,
When they stare at you exclusively
With unsure trust so close to embarrassment,
With unprepossessing outrageous bravery
That seems too pure and fragile to be real,
When their voices quiver but their hands are poised,
When they face you in motionless eager exposure,
Like three dimensions spread out into two,
Flat, illuminated, stark in simplicity,
All mystery gone, all masks removed,
When they hand you the flower of their hidden longing,
When they pray you'll hold so gently
Their gift, their treasure, their plea…

For then, and *only* then,
You will know them.
In that singular moment
The world of another person is open, clear.
You can see your way through,
Every part's well-lit,
No labyrinths hide the buried secrets,
No catacombs shelter corners in the dark;
For once, someone's *real*,
And incredibly delicate, vulnerable, soft,
Defenseless beneath your ambiguous power.
The consummate decision's in your lap then,
For the defenselessness makes them
Too *absolutely* real,
Too momentously alive in this most tender
Of existential and terrifying moments.

And you'll want to relent,

Forgo the blatant advantage and strength,
Give up all strategy,
Pretend that rules, compromise and loss,
Never diminish our noblest dreams.
There in that instant you'll know
A person's meaning, the truth, revealed.
For once you'll genuinely *see* someone,
Ruthlessly disrobed by a gesture, by a line,
By three little words that tear down walls,
Shatter boundaries, fling away diversions,
In a sudden unmasking of life's
Covert and momentous occasions—
This unabashed gift of another being,
This horrendous responsibility,
This flagrant trust, this ridiculous hope,
This laying of one's life on a razor's line—
Absurd! Nonsense!
A monument to stupidity—
Yet a monument to faith, dreams, hope.

And then…
You're *it*.
You hold this childlike flower, this bud.
Life's *yours* then.
And what you do with it
Will determine
Just how "absolutely real"
You
Can be.

Figure In a Landscape

Last night I dreamt of the Spiral Palms.
And the joy and wonder of that lost time
Welled up inside me like an ocean at night,
All I had felt, and now felt again.

Every detail was there in my dream:
The blade-like fronds, the coiled trunks,
The sky like metal and the ocean like fog.
And you, in unexpected low golden light,
Sitting with your back to me, your hair enflamed,
Absorbed by what you saw while trying to paint it,
Trying to capture and free it at once.

You're out there, I see you,
Red-haired artist in a sun's level blaze,
Capturing moments you slice from eternity,
Your pictures like lamps, dragon lanterns,
Hidden sanctuaries of colors that breathe,
Awaking the inhabitant of every dark tree,
The clouds in the interiors of crystal-ball planets,
Spinning fire rings, living vapors,
A torus of rainbow planetary mist.

All these are you, memories of you.

There in the middle of this planetary stage,
Centered with your back to me,
Deliberating, painting, amid caverns of ice,
Blue inner peaks and fragmented suns,
You watch the mountains
And thus try to climb them,
Know them in uniquely aesthetic ways,
Re-define them, in order to create them.

You're the woman in the landscape,
The woman against the sky.
I learned to see based on your eyes,

The universe reached me
Once it came through you:
Frame, composition, texture, light—
My spaceship named desire,
My planetary lover.

I cannot tell the story of you,
How we shattered expectation,
Found happiness in duress,
Discovered so much
By touching all things,
Lost every definition
By losing ourselves
In the regard of each other,
In our mutual absorption,
Our sublimation into scenery.

And I cannot tell
How I lost you then,
So many years ago.

Yet, last night,
You were there in my dream,
Figure emergent from vermilion deserts,
Chandeliered peaks, caverns of glass,
Multi-colored glaciers bleeding painted streams,
Sitting with your back to me
And touched in lowlight,
Watching the landscape
And trying to drink it,
Trying to be subject and object at once.
Found, and lost,
So many years ago.

You came to me
From illuminated forests
With iridescent flowers and vines of flame.
You emerged from a world called Aquamarine
With its turquoise growth and emerald caves.
Or we dabbled with heat in a tropical realm

Under fattened leaves and caressing moss,
Beside leglike roots and limbs like arms—
Where you sketched, walked with me,
Eager for my tales of untouched planets,
Made rapt by the backgrounds I so loved,
All once mine.

I made you my assistant
Though I needed none then.
I work best alone,
And yet you asked,
Your longing too strong.
I soon said yes.
And, for a while,
We lived in surprise,
Spectacle, sensation.

Then you found others.
You went their ways
Though I could read your regrets.
You realized your task
Required an ascension
That I could not share,
Many choices, different ties.
I wished you well, thinking then that
Landscapes were better than people.
It was what I taught you.
I got back what I gave.

Until, last night,
There, in my dream…

Was the woman,
The setting,
The longing…

Mileen.

No Frontiers

If I find you—

The place will be inward
As well as out,
No borders, no screens,
You and I
And it together
With waterfalls and caves,
The earth like a room,
With lush green leaves
In pads of leather,
Suede and velvet,
Fur on branches,
Flaking sleeves
Of soft scaly bark,
Where the stars will dazzle
To remind me of you.

There we'll partake,
There feed and grow,
Nest, be still,
Be other in extension
And reflected and found:
In that realm, that planet,
Where you and I
And all else that lives
Will be less than one
But more than two,
In this world unbounded—

If I find you.

Conversation in a Darkened Spaceship

When you wanted me to hold you,
I joked, "You feel lost?
But you're the most 'located'
Person I know."
You said, "At one time."
I didn't have an answer.

The ship moved on
Through its private darkness,
Ports open to the stars.
In its dim interior,
Candles burned.

We worried our time
With frets, false pride:
"It's larger than us now."
"Nothing was larger
Than us before."
"We *were* quite a couple."
"Yes. I remember."

Haloes of silence
Filled candle-lit darkness.

Words kept us solvent,
Brave, informed,
Utilized, functional.
"We were so compatible."
"If we broke," you said,
"We easily could put ourselves
Together again."
"You came in one piece—
'No construction required.'"
And you said, slowly,
"It wasn't always that easy."

Again, the silence.

You claimed, "Space is terrible,
Cold, empty, radiated, dead."

"Don't sugar-coat it," I refuted,
Irony always my first defense,
"You don't like the stars?"
"They're just imitations."
"But you can't see in time-space.
The ports' electronics
Have to reproduce them."
"They're still disappointing.
It's all so fake."
Again, I had no answer.

Then we talked of threats,
What still could endanger us,
The "mission," the Clip—
The obsessed, the pursued,
The space in between—
"But," I argued, "what *we* have is bigger."
"That's us, all right!"
"Mutual fortress against the Big Dark!"
"I do think we're something."

Then, a long pause.

"We say that so *carefully*."
"We say that so *guard*edly."

The ship plowed on,
Carrying its private
Well-wrought darkness.
In its ports, fake stars.
In its one warmed room
A flurry of candles,
Dim small flames.

"Let's hold each other," I said.
We both now had said it.

One tiny spaceship,
Almost adrift,
In large,
Open,
Inward,
Outer space.

The Last Farewell

Goodbye, once more,
Not to you but to us,
To what we had together,
To what we briefly made.

They say that explorers
Need to be unselfish,
And I believe we were.
We wanted only each other,
For whatever fine reasons
Each of us still believed.
Were we falsely deserving
Of our choice, our chance?
Of the many clear delights
We achieved together?

I feel no hope now.
I expect nothing.
Yet I can't abandon thoughts
Of what we were together.
I regret that our desire
Simply failed to persist.

So goodbye, my beloved.
Farewell, once more,
As an unexpected irony
Weighs down what I feel:
I never once thought
We'd break so clearly,
Practically, quickly,
And so well.

Yet, please know,
My love for you
Was a prayer.
And each day,
Each morning,
Each night,
I prayed.

The Touch

In flight:

An aircar
In stupendous isolation.
Inside, a partnering,
A sharing in the dark,
A prelude or slope
Of an upward swirl
Into fresh and growing
New identities.
He feels himself
Becoming lost
In her.

They land by glaciers
Amid ocean spray,
Ice-fields breaking
In thaw and growth,
Like his own private self
Awakening after misery.
He's suddenly found her.
He wants to lavish
In these mutual, budding,
Exuberant moments.

They see living crystal,
Walking flames,
A river serpent
With a rainbow tail.
He knows she thinks
All life is holy,
That everyone lives
In a sacred landscape.
He follows her words
But not all of what she says.
He listens to her voice
And watches her lips.

There's too much realism
Beside him for ideas.
He wants only her.

Icicled trees
By a frozen lake,
Hard thick cushions
Of snow-covered ground.
Even in this blank
Star-torn darkness,
Where all things sensual
Are brittle and cold,
They seize this tender
Proffered moment,
This exquisite chance
To glide together.

He slides his finger
Down her face
In a raw sensual
Arc of longing.
He touches her lips,
Lightly, lightly.
His finger trembles.
Thus his hands
Destroy all art,
Replace design
With pure sensation—
To love her in a language
That came before words.

They kiss, they caress.
They are part of the landscape,
They charge it with
Intimate sensory meaning,
The iced trees
And the glazed snow,
The hill-like cliffs
And distant mountains.
They consume its otherness,
Collect its broken parts,

Participate in
An ongoing creation.
They empower this world's
Longing to be.

Though the frozen trees
Resemble claws,
She says she would
Hug the snowy boughs.
Such incongruity
Makes sense to him.
He's seen how she can
Destroy frontiers.
It's where he wants to go.

He would lose himself
In this new panorama—
This blanketing frost,
These knife-edged slopes—
If just to kiss her
In the silence once more.
Their world needs nothing
To animate itself.
They two are enough.

They leave, she pilots.
Her pondering is frank,
Her moves confident,
Her dark eyes
No longer self-conscious.
He loves the coils
Of her black braid,
Its interwoven ropes of hair—
To her, it's only functional,
To him, a delight.

She longs for her planet
To be set free,
To unleash its myths
And buried archetypes.

He believes in her,
Wants to help her.
But she *is* her planet,
It needs nothing else.
They hold hands
As she flies the aircar,
He looks out the window
Until she asks,
"What do you see out there?"
He responds, "You."

They annihilate distance
As they inhabit each other.
Flying, she can't see him,
Only fingertips touch,
But they're fully aware
Of a joint presence.
The vehicle is filled
With their knowledge
Of each other,
Their unspoken
Rhetoric of love.

They look ahead
To where they are going,
Not across to what they are.
Each other's eyes
Would melt themselves now.
With his hand in hers
Their fingers speak.
They make new rapture
With this soft-handed love,
With the subtle intoxication
Of touch.

He wants to define her,
Follow her outline
With his hands,
Trace and sculpt her,
Make more alive

Her lean form,
Instill her flesh
With pulse, charge,
A novel awareness,
Arouse her skin
To new organs of sense,
Open her to endless
Physical worlds,
Permeate her,
Flow inside her,
Inhabit each nerve
And fill each pore—
All this while in flight,
His thoughts roaming
Above the dark
And shadow-filled land.

Later, he'll caress
The memory of her,
That frosty night
By the crusted lake,
Under stars and aurora
In the falling snow.
But he's afraid his recalling it
Will wear it down, rub it thin,
That he'll cherish it to death
And suck the magic dry.

As they near the station,
They both know
They must be careful.
The cultural guards,
Even the military,
Might cause them concern,
See her as a traitor,
Him an outsider,
Not part of their "destiny,"
Of their long sustained
Mythological Dream.
They'll fear he's pulling her

Out of their future,
Trying to change her.
And they'd be right.
He wants to love her.
He thinks he's succeeding.

In the barracks:

They now feel uncomfortable.
They don't know how
To approach each other,
When to be formal
Yet intimate too.
An invisible storm
Is always brewing.
They're too aware
Of how they appear.
They imagine others
Watching them, tailing them,
Maybe even wanting
To imitate them.

He fears her rejection,
A sudden ethical,
Planetological
Or historical wall,
A socially generated
Tactful retreat,
An abandonment
Of all they've done together.
He looks for signs of it.
He over-interprets.

They're too speculative
With each other.
Their reactions are "mixed."
One part of him feels guilt
While another part wants more.
He asks her for a sign to know
Which feeling dominates in her.

He's being too desperate.
He shows it, a fault.

When they were alone
On their excursion
Across wilderness,
They could say anything.
But now a small word,
A gesture, a line,
Might seem too significant.
They show less of what they feel,
But they imagine more.

After they're parted
By planning sessions,
Wartime agendas,
He awaits the sound
Of her entering a room,
A time electric with possible wonder.
Will she come to see him first
Or will he go to her?
When will their words
Take on double meaning?
Will their eagerness counter
The outward restraints?
Though they've grown so near,
They too easily feel
They could slip out of touch.

So many are the steps
And missteps of love.
How does one simplify
Crude complexity,
Say the right phrase,
Make the right move?
She tells him she needs a "fix."
He asks if she means a "repair"
Or a "pick-me-up"?
"A dose," she says.
He first feels joy.

Then, he's not sure.

If they're in a public room
They keep the doors open,
Let the eyes of others
Provide their restraint.
It takes will to leave a spot
Where they're together.
They stare at each other
With vivid intensity,
The longing palpable.
Their hands seek freedom
To reach across a gap.
They want to kiss,
Cling, caress,
Dive headlong into each other.
But they just stare.
The room, silent,
Reverberates
With longing,
All of it theirs.

For a long time
They do not kiss
But they still feel close.
Only their eyes
Make love to each other.
It's dreamlike,
But not *Dream*like.
They don't fit
Her world's folklore.
Pioneers don't.
He's not surprised.

Did it really happen?
Did they just share
So much cherished time?
But constraining themselves
Makes unreality grow.
Love seems imaginary.
They feel they're playing parts,

That the station is a theater
Ruled by inertia.
They want to overstep
All social rules,
They know only want.
They've left their universe
And destroyed the norm.

They dine with others
But feel separate and apart.
He can only leave her
By staying with her longer.
Her eyes above her glass
Are almost predatory,
As if reaching for a miracle
That *can* be obtained.
They join hands beneath the table.
Could she possibly want him
As much as he wants her,
Now, this instant?

Time leaves them
(He now gets their philosophy),
Bringing into focus
Their attention, their regard.
She says his stare
Is obviously a lover's,
That anyone at the table
Would read it and know.
He becomes insecure.
They can't finish the meal.
They replace hunger with desire.
In all this light, in this busy hall,
They're still in their own
Separate world,
Their binary planet.

In her room:

They pass through the door

Not caring who sees them.
The line between their eyes
Is taut as a tightrope.
They are close now, they touch.
He's amazed at how quickly
They fall together,
Into hands, clutching, holds,
Embrace.

Their moves are tentative,
He seeks first
The depths of her eyes,
The shadows in the loops
Of her black hair.
Her braid uncouples,
Unwinds its DNA swirls
In sumptuous abandon—
In a call, an invitation,
To darkness and light,
To all backgrounds
To join in their love,
To share their singular
And new hallowed game.

They sense, from outside,
The scattered beacons
Of this world's night,
Lining the cliffs above the crater.
They are now lovers
On this strange lost planet,
She from its ground,
He from its sky,
But they don't feel like
Any legend or myth.
They grip each other
As if riding a maelstrom.

His hands become charged
As they near her skin.
Desire heats, surrounds,

Cocoons them.
They give birth to a new
Cross-planetary pleasure,
Her skin touches back
As his hands grope.
Boundaries vanish.

He's not surprised
By the depth of her passion,
The well of dark flame
Inside her—he saw it
When she spoke of desires
She had for her world.
He longs to inhabit
The artistry of her body,
Of her mind, her life.
He swims to her, downriver,
In this flood of longing,
Meets her in these eager eddies.
He's shaken, tossed.
Then afterward, beached—
Clinging, holding,
Arriving together,
Carried to safety,
Victims of themselves,
Paired survivors
Of dangerous encounters.

His finger again touches her lips—
She opens, takes it in,
Sucks hard and takes another.
He slides his hand along her thighs,
Her long smooth inner lengths,
Till he reaches the gap
Where his finger enters,
Two, then three.
Parts of both hands now inside her—
He wants to become her,
Lift her, turn her,

Make orgasm from within.

Her face lies beneath him,
Settled now, sedate,
Like a newfound
But satisfied country,
A landscape fully
Aware of itself.
She fills his vision.
Her expression's like a pool
Of clear, pure water
That he wants to lift
And pour over his face,
Feel its promise, elation, joy.

Her mouth is open,
Her breathing deep,
Her eyes eager
As if ready to love again,
To become in touch
With her world, with him.
Her face is only
Inches away—
This is when
He loves her the most.

He hears her writhe
In their broken silence,
Finds the life seething inside her,
He wants to claim,
Develop, unearth,
The landscape of her,
The topography of her,
Find his own secret Alchera,
Reach the planet that speaks to him,
That touches back.

He dreams of spending
Long nights with her,
Riding the endless waves of her,

His hands on her skin
Awaking an ancient
Forgotten awareness.
The sounds she makes
Are more felt than heard.
She's always in motion,
In constant sensory give and take.
She swallows the sounds
Of yet another climax—
She tries for quiet
In this, their storm.
It is impossible, not to be.

As he lies beside her,
Contained in her,
Their mutual coupling
Finally spent,
He, in a light consolation,
Or jest,
Presses his finger
Into the palm of her hand—
A spastic motion,
A semiotic imitation
Of climax.

She leans back
Across his legs,
He kisses her gently-held face.
Though her culture
Doesn't believe in time,
They both feel it passing now,
He swims in its gentle waters,
Holding her body in his arms.
They stare into each other,
Across each other,
Invading, absorbing,
Entering with their eyes,
Reminding with their hands.

The aftermath:

What will happen now?

How can they relate
To the others around them?
Will he stay, or will she go?
What choices await them?
What world will they inhabit?
Annulus? Alchera? Old Earth?
His barren hollowed asteroid?
Maybe we should stop,
He almost thinks.
But he can't, he won't.
He'd rather abandon home.
He wants this new world—
This world of her.

He's terrified
That his looking ahead,
With his expectations,
Will become replaced
With only looking back
In awe,
Or worse, in fear.
The future frightens him.
Yet it beckons.

Then her people come
To take away both of them.
There's much to be done.
He has to leave on a mission
(So he can return to them).
He must become free
(So he can reclaim her).
He needs to bury himself
(So he can find himself.
And then…find her.)

He awakens to a dream—
Mylia! Chasing her!
Rush, before she's gone.

Stolen Moment

I leave, I'm alone,
I'm adrift on Homeworld,
Left with only thoughts.

How can I paint her,
Conjure her from memory,
Produce my failed
If timid copy?
Outline her shoulders,
Her neck, her face,
Highlight the glints
In her sable hair,
Relate the sound
Of her voice,
Her passion,
Depict her ardent
And storm-fed eyes?

I cannot paint her.
I can only love her.
That is my statement.

I want my gift to her
To be her own true self.
I want her to cherish
What she is in my eyes.
I want my masterpiece
To be my love for her.

Written In Prison

Longing is not proper,
And desire's out of the question,
So, arms folded, feelings held in,
I make no outward sign
That I await my return to you.
The guards don't know
I can cultivate restraint.

By the time I'm with you
It well might be Spring
(I'm sure your world
Provides such a season),
And the lush buds
Will unfold, abundant,
Eager to greet you
In the way I cannot,
Hug you in warmth,
Touch you with joy,
As I, "behind bars,"
Near drunk with fear
Of never escaping,
Cannot now achieve.

Of all things deprived me
I miss most your smile.
Spring longs to find you
For it knows you add to it,
The season's bright growth
Will throng to greet you,
The trees, blossoms,
All things yearning
Toward you, toward life.

As I,
Like small violets,
Do.

The Woman In the Tree

As night fell and winds rose,
I heard a tragic siren call.
I raced from my hut to the ocean cliff...

Where I saw a white translucent glow,
Impaled, entwined, in a bare-branched tree.
A white creature in black moon dark,
Delicate, captive, clothes knifed by the limbs,
Half unformed, indeterminate life,
With features in flux and face in pain,
A child-like wraith, a creature of the wind,
Snagged, un-free, flailing with need,
Against the confining clutching embrace
Of this spindly, witch's, wooden claw.

And I, caring, plucked at the bonds,
Disengaged the white wrap,
Tugged and yanked until I held—
The woman in the tree.
She had called. I came,
To this elf, spirit, transient of the storm,
So thin of substance, so freed of weight,
So filled with desire that screamed
In her sharp and determined eyes,
That begged to be onward, to leave, to soar—
Her pale arm pointed the way,
Her long hair lined the wind with black.

And thus, in seeing, such need, such longing,
I—let her go, let be, let fly.
The buoyant air drew her swiftly off.
Her shrinking, pale, luminescent form
Bounced in the torrent, withdrew,
Disappeared....

The sea tossed, the sky closed.
Alone I stood on that cliff unmoving,

Throughout a long and emptied night,
Till dawn's indifferent and pale light came,

And bleak…
Day.

One Good Memory

A comparison
For you
In that simple
White dress:

A child
In a school
For angels,
At recess.

IV. Tales of Old Earth

Ruby Beach

It rained there
(It always did),
And wet beads made ghosts
In our hair.

We felt time leave
In a shrug of withdrawal,
To some other sea
And some other where.

Magenta kelp and a purple sea-star
Gemmed the wet tarpaulin-smooth stones,
Garnets amid steel.
And lines of birds,
In quiet, winged, far exaltation
Skimmed the calm and crushed-ice air.

Heaps of shredded, storm-wrought logs,
Glazed in iron, white-orange, or red,
Lay before trees, preoccupied, tall,
That faced the shore with a pensive,
Secret, evasive, stare.

All things veiled were saturated, damp,
With panes of cloud in primeval chill,
Drowning the day.
They wrung me, stained me,
Watered me with longing
To write and to pray:
Lord, it's not *fair*
To be here—
And it there.

So wet, so gray,

And so far away.

The Haunted

She stands on a barren cliff and stares
To the drowned lands far in the west,
The sunken cities and forsaken kingdoms,
Where she, daughter of an ancient race,
Once stole secrets—with her helpmate lover—
From cruel tyrants to give to the oppressed.
But, caught, she was tried and banished,
Flung to this land-gripped sullen world,
Where, later, she could only watch in horror
As her Atlantean continent—and her lover—
Sank in disaster beneath the gray sea.
So that now, she stares,
Left with nothing for her endless desire.

And I, from a meager nearby village
Of poor simple folk, barely a man,
Not near enough worthy, watch her in pain,
As she, unaware of me, watches the sea.

Oh I know she's unreachable,
Of a world not my own,
I realize my longing is naïve and selfish.
But say *not* I'm afflicted, say not that fate
Has placed her here for only the torture
Of my hopeless love.
No. I believe—I declare!—
That the *living*, and not ghosts,
Determine our obsessions.

We are not led by spirits unkind.
We *choose* our haunts.

And thus…
She is mine.

Black Canary's Blue Song

Sorry, dear Oliver,
But we've no time tonight.
Don't follow me, don't watch me,
And don't get in my way.
I've got darker tasks than you tonight.
Leave me to my own private vengeance.
Male-bond with Hal, relive your past,
The noble years of crying and raving
You went through then.
He needs you. He's sad.

Not that you're very helpful or sensitive.
You'll complain he's "not a man,"
That he should learn from you.
But don't try to make him an extension of yourself.
And don't do the same to me, Ollie dear.
Don't preach at me, talk at me,
Formulate what I am and then impose it.
I have no time for such mind-games tonight.
I've discovered something dreadful, you see:
We *are* vulnerable.
Superheroes *can* be hurt—emotionally!
That's how Luthor got to me, the bastard,
Leering with his threats,
"You will be my *instrument*.
You will be my *tool*.
And then...you will be *mine*."

I don't yet know what he was planning
Except to cause pain—to me, to you.
Maybe he guessed that Batman would find me,
Take me to his "Batcave" to fix my wounds.
And that there, yes, we would make love.
I'm sorry, Oliver.
But yes, we did it, the dark knight and I.
And don't get that marble look on your face.
I still don't *know* him. I insisted he wear his mask.
I wanted no ties, no empathy at all.
We were just two soldiers comforting each other.

He's much too careful to fall for me.
He knows all about being vulnerable already.
He lost Robin, remember. And something else,
But I couldn't tell what.

And thus Luthor hurts *you,* through me.
Do you understand now?
I know these emotions better than you.
You always run and hide from your feelings
And leave me to clean up after.
That's what Luthor is using against us.
He got to Hal through Carol like that
(For god's sake, watch what you say to him).
And don't look so pained and sullen now.
You've made me an "instrument" too, you know,
The way of maintaining *your* function and goal.

But I refuse all subservience now.
I'm tired of being the victim,
The object of other people's actions and designs.
Yes, I know you love me,
But—love is *easy*—cheap, undemanding.
And I don't need single-minded worship tonight.
It's just another form of debasement anyway.
And I can't help it if all this hurts you.
I've been hurt too, you know.
I had sex with Batman for more reasons than one.

So…sorry, Ollie.
No fishnets tonight.
There still will be time for you and me,
But not yet, not now.
I've got "business" tonight,
My own personal reprisal and payback.
Let me be. Back off.
And know, tall brooding
Superhero of mine,
For tonight, for *this* night,
And for maybe nights after,
The *Darkness*
Is mine.

Death Valley and Las Vegas

The colors of the West
Can be seen in just the names:
Red Rock, Gold Canyon,
Chocolate Mountain, Pink Cliffs.
"Land of the Sleeping Rainbow" indeed.
Images in words make new accords,
And poetry melds the great divide.

Some places jar, shock your awareness,
Leave a sublime reverent silence.
Death Valley is almost subterranean,
An alien planet torn open to the sun.
You descend—you *descend!*—
And experience peaks in hot low depths.
The grandeur's appalling, like a lover's slap,
And catharsis arrives only after you leave.

But then there's Las Vegas,
So incredibly nearby,
Where artificial light
And exploitation rule,
Where depletion beckons,
Where huge casinos
Like gravity-wells
Suck you into slots,
Where everything is human,
All *too* human.
(Or maybe just capitalist,
But…I have my doubts.)

The desert, instead, floods you
With dryness—it burns, overwhelms.
It's other, beyond you, in a different Time.
It doesn't know you, it doesn't care.
Our own worst habits suckle us in town,
But, unfinished, Death Valley lies raw.
Creation stopped there all too soon—

The rocks discarded, the salt spilled,
The ground unclean, the water poison,
The sky malevolent, the colors abstracted
Beyond laws of art, clashing, overdone.
Extravagant. Absurd.
Utterly *in*human.

Oh, how I loved it!

In the City of Godzilla

The curved towers are ribs of bone.
Talons break the earth's skin
And are used as elevators, or spiral stairs.
Windows puncture gargantuan teeth,
Then shrink as they near the sharp tips,
Like apartments for wolves,
Then rodents, then fleas.

Once living scales pave "cobblestone" streets,
Hardened and glazed by fashionable sandals.
The eyes, once sinister, are obsidian domes
That house arenas for concerts and plays.
And the doughty old monster's blue-flame breaths
Shoot discharge columns for furnaces in power plants.
Hardened saliva makes spider-web walkways,
And the great bugle ears are now warehouse doors.

Though some say the city's odors are strong,
No one denies the living space is cheap.
The stylized carcass makes upscale flats
Where fingernails are skylights, eyelashes whips,
And the gums avant-garde settees and stools.
The radiation wars that brought down this colossus
Made its corpse surprisingly accommodating—
For the kinky-chic trendsetting crowds
Whose victors conquer in more ways than one.
The creature's death, once quintessential,
Is hardly slighted by becoming architectural.

And yet, Mothra,
The one-time dragon's old close friend,
Once as colossal and fearsome as he,
But reduced now too by the atomic blasts
To a size no more than a true moth's (pre-nuclear),
Glides down from the still glowing sky
And alights, gently, on a once commanding
And deadly thumb, where he ponders,

With sorrow, how so much has changed.

And he dreams of seeing yet once more
His massive pal, reveling and striding,
With claws like backhoes and thighs like whales,
As he squashes the squalid soft-fleshed maggots
Who now—how it pains him!—put doilies on incisors,
Fragile glass lamps in cavernous pores,
And wall-hanging peace signs
On his often bloodied—
But proud—
Rebel skin.

The Rainbow Way

We returned—
They called us "Nomads."
But "Wind People" seems best,
For the world is inhabited
By spirits, like us,
Who cross landscapes by day
And motel-rooms by night,
Who are pilgrims in transit,
Followers of seasons,
Cycles, and change,
On the go, restless,
Holding only to each other.

We move on, move by,
Under suns made of turquoise
And moons of white quartz,
In legendary lands
Of silver-faced gods,
Where the north is black
With storm clouds thick,
Where the east is white
And lightning fraught,
Where the south is blue
Like the awning of sky,
And where the west is yellow,
Ancient home of the sun.

Holy People in passing,
We haunt the sacred Earth.
We're dragonflies by day
And bat-messengers by night,
Dry-land nomads
And signifying ghosts,
On the Navajo colored-bridge
That rims sand-paintings
With light-beams astray—
For though here,

We are *there*…

On the old,
All-sanctioned,
And dry,
Rainbow Way.

The Spell

He said,
"Earthbound witch,
Was it you or I
Or what we did together
That brought down the moon
To lie with us tonight?"

And she said,
"Oh, silly!—
It's just a hole in the roof.
Be happy it didn't rain!
Though my gown on the hay
With your bodkin and boots
Did make a winning
Renaissance tableau."

And he said,
"Was it you who gathered
All the bright stars above
And then inspired them,
By what we did?
Made them feel sad longing
For the life they can't have?"

And she said,
"Well, we do owe them *something!*
Since the moon did shed
Its fine romantic glow—
Violet, dim red, old soft ivory—
On my shadowed skin
And your smooth hairy flank."

And he said,
"But it's you, Earth spirit,
Who rules deep space,
Swirls the nebulae
With soft magic hands—

To ignite!—
With those eyes."

And she said,
"Oh, my dear, you *are* so sweet!
But I do this just for you,
Build castles, breach walls,
Make you knight and I queen,
Lace our love with this fine
Exotic historical aplomb."

And thus, satisfied,
He dons doublet and sword,
She bodice and cloak,
To emerge hidden in Medieval mist,
He to his Harley,
I-70 to Weirton in far West Virginia,
And she to her broomstick—
Night flight to Fanghorn,
Black Mountain of Magic,
In the north.

Nosferatu

Your nails are too long,
Your teeth are too bright,
Your hunchbacked shadow
Falls blacker than midnight.

Stand off from bloodlust,
Trade red eyes for blue,
Find another, or *any* life,
Nosferatu.

Your ears are too sharp,
Your mouth's made of fangs,
Your hands are like spiders,
Your eyebrows overhang.

Discard your immortality!
It's what you ought to do,
For saving you gets harder,
Nosferatu.

The Fall

Spring's Elizabethan, summer is Greek,
Winter's a stark Medieval Romanesque.
But autumn? Ah, *Romantic* is the fall.

Old cathedrals in sad ruination are perfect
For autumn's fell tinted shades.
It's not real Gothic's religious sublime
But the loss of all that certainty instead.
Though the march of Western Cultural Traditions
Might well reflect Earth's flowing seasons,
Fall transcends both theater and history.

The leaves tumble like angels in exile
From plum-blue heaven to yellow-red earth:
Ripped skins, gilt dreams, frayed scabs, drops of blood,
Scarred little Satans in flames of descent.
Summer's soft embroidered green is charred
In Beethoven's surging last movements,
In lurking gray mist and cool colored steam.
Limbs of trees grow crackling and bare
Under frightful, hard, Lovecraftian skies.
Stars stare and threaten only in autumn:
In winter, they're candles; in summer, lamps.
But in fall they splinter, sharpen, ache,
Like pin-heads of sparks seeking bare eyes,
While demons of Cthulhu hide in piled leaves.
And the setting, now weary of life's high demands,
Sheds, weeps, strips cloaks, and dies,
Burned-up, burnt out, in a landfall of decay—
All parties gone, only shreds of life left,
Crepe-paper droppings, colored wrappers, leaves.

The lone brooding Romantics would have loved it,
This wreckage, this wilderness, this silence and heap,
These stark decomposing supernatural halls,
Where shards of colored glass lace the ground
Like discarded, transitory, decadent gems,

Testaments to life and warmth departed,
In a macabre excess of colored debris,
Of exquisite death, a festival of death.
Think of them, these posturing agonized players,
These lonely Romantics in lonelier shades,
Who sought for certainty when the galaxies fell
Like careening rose-windows on parched dead fields—
Who grew sullen, frenzied, ecstatic at what they saw—

That in slow-tinted autumn comes
The fall.

Wonder Woman Speaks to Superman

What are they, Clark?
These people of Earth
We protect, and love?
Why are we so like them
And yet never quite the same?
I'm a god, you're an alien,
But we're not inhuman.
They place us always
Above or beneath them,
Yet never quite *like* them.
Are we nearing what they are?
Growing more worldly?
Or are they becoming gods?
I don't know. I'm confused.

What do they see in us?
Why do they make us
Their conceived ideals
As if they're incapable
Of ever doing good?
Why do they distrust
Their own innocence—
Why do they require it,
And then destroy it?
Why are they so cruel
And emotionally indulgent,
Insensitive to what they feel
In others, *and* themselves?
Why is their potential
So marred by their being
Both fragile and callous—
Like over-rich children
Too wary of looking bad.
I pity them and love them,
And yet they frighten me.
They claim they love us,

But…I have my doubts.

Why do they say—
Say right to our faces!—
"Only a god or a superman
Could be so pure"?
Why can't *we* be real too?
Why is everything defined
By *their* definitions?
So what if you're a "boy scout."
Am I wrong to be a virgin?
I'm from a lost race
And you a lost world,
So we never allow ourselves
To be as smug as they—
We're too responsible, too alone,
Too self-conscious of being a deity
Or an orphan from space
(Which, I swear, they hold against us),
Their attitudes so dominating
They can make even us
Feel awkward and shy.

In all my fantasies about you, Clark,
We never reach a sexual love.
We kissed once—in such timid splendor—
As if frightened of *their* cascades of emotion.
But do we really need their tired context
In order to be ourselves?
Why are we so frightened
Just to be together, to go on a "date"?
We could fly around Jupiter,
Skate on Saturn's rings,
Walk the length of Valles Marineris
And swim in the volcano pools of Io.
But we never do.
Earth might be threatened.
We're too self-aware
Of our inherited sacred duties,
Too afflicted with goodness.

We bury our brash desiring selves
And say, unselfishly,
"Some other time...not now."

But I wish—just once—
Oh, Clark, forgive me—
To feel simple, yet needed.
I want pleasure, not ecstasy,
Not catastrophic deliverance
But small daily joys.
Come on, "man of steel,"
Answer me this query, this desire!
When will we *know*—know for certain—
That all we do is pertinent, authentic?
When will *we* at last become
As self-satisfied, and assured, as they?
When will we prove ourselves—
To ourselves, *for* ourselves?
When will we shed this tired role of savior
And finally relax in complacent ease,
Console ourselves with kindness, softness,
Even "normalness" too?
Oh, Clark, "God on Earth,"
When will we, as they—
As all such humans seem to do—
Feel childlike, natural, simple,
Uncalled for,
And yet,
Still valid?

Rain People

Umbrellas they use
Not as tents from torrents,
But more as disguises,
Masks or screens,
And their turned-up collars
And shut-in coats
Are allies of grayness—
The element becomes them
As they walk, not rush,
Through rain-filled, lamp-struck,
Fugitive streets.

Or you see them in windows
Looking out at the damp,
From behind wet streams
And flat running panes,
Their faces pensive,
Secret, withdrawn—
They don't mind isolation
If they command good views.
They're not spies, but they watch—
Like veiled wanderers
With sharpened looks,
Not aliens but apart,
In a subtly chosen exile
From crowds, from the throng's
Taut and self-indulgent play.
They touch, but don't bind.
Their pleasant hello
Is a qualified good-bye,
And a soft "By your leave"
Means a clear "I must away."

Like the impartial penetrating rain,
They've looked into shadows,
They miss nothing,
They know that survival

Can be harmless, but hardened,
Unnoticed, yet real.
And so, invisible,
Neither far away
Nor close to their homes,
In the tall wet curtains
Of fine falling rain,
They are secret as mist,
And as strong as the sea.

And at times,
They are you.

And at times,
They are me.

Dracula's Woman

I am a blood-red rose
And you are the black thorn-bush
That holds me.

The snow where I was left,
Discarded and forgotten,
Is white, virgin.
And you, a tendril
Charred black as night,
Crept to me, touched me.

Your handling is delicate
But your thorns are sharp,
A pain I welcome,
Ancient, profound,
Redolent of stark
And brutal insight.

Only you break my skin,
Dissolve boundaries
And make me you.
I look down at my open
Gauze-white dress
And see one Rorschach
Blossom of blood.
My blood. *Your* blood.

You are not death
But spell-bound life,
Vast heart-beat
In a world anemic.
You erase me,
Make me pure.
In your dependence
You dominate me;
And I, nurturer—
Mother, mistress,

Daughter, and wife—
Am essential, fulfilled,
Immaculate,
Pristine.

My lips are black,
My eyes a fevered
Desirous blue,
Like cold moons
In dim ivory clouds.
My snow-gown is spotted
With dried petal-flames,
Scarlet, crimson,
Memories of you.

We are complete now.
You need not seek me
For I am your extension,
A burning red sun
In your bottomless night,
A rose…on sable.

I am the red star
And you the black hole.
My plasma flames
Make red oil trails
That spiral—
Into you.

Reach for me in silence
With black moon-wings,
Fly me over countries
Of the meek and craven.
Loft me, save me,
Hide me from light…

The light that is pain,
So unlike your pain.

Yes.

We are one,
Demon and lover.
Oh, yes,
My devourer!
In loud black silence
And endless night
I say yes...

Yes.

Night and the Phantom

A woman with three kids, two dogs, a house,
And a husband whose paunch will never fit again
That gold-braid uniform from the "Masquerade" number,
Hardly feels like an "Angel of Music."

Oh, I still hum in the shower,
Conduct Sunday school jams,
Advise local musical plays,
And remember how I rocked
My babies to sleep with lullabies
So tender and soft.
But, as for being a "divine muse,"
An object of secret impassioned desire
By a genius whose song—and love—was me,
Well, life *is* a web of compromise,
A withering, a paring, a shaving of what's best
To allow survival of the resultant lean.
(The flesh grows soft as the thoughts grow hard.)
Oh I'm satisfied, quite well, content,
Less adventurous but more safe.
I have solid back-up, I provide support.
I can say I'm happy and not have to joke.

And yet…
At times, when I walk late at night,
On slightly misted lamp-lit streets,
I hear from the shadows,
In theatrical strains,
In brief, fleeting, fugitive airs,
Your voice…my Phantom,
Fragments and hints of your operatic song.
I know I'm imagining, but conviction's so sweet.
I persuade myself you're near, wanting me still,
Yearning, seeking, intent with desire.
There's comfort in believing
That messages in secret
Hang in night airs and are sent,

Direct, though indirect, to me.

But then, in a wave of predictable pain,
I realize—I remember—
At least one of us no longer exists.
Our lovely music of the night is done,
Is beyond resurrection, is silent, still,
Is only a relic on the dusty, backward,
And crowded shelves of forsaken pasts.

And thus, saddened, I walk on, alone,
(Except for increasingly distant Raoul—
Does he too feel the withdrawal of romance?),
A smile hiding my discomfort, penciled on my face.
And I think: Life too is a music of the night,
But it ever withdraws before the clarity of day,
From a dawn persistent, relentless, cold,
From a tyrant logic that bleaches the dark.

And so, my fancy, my one dear treasure,
My ever withdrawing fading dream,
I must say, in truth,
In all well-lit but ugly truth,
That I know, sweet Phantom,
Beloved, my own,
I know
(Alas!)
You do not sing for me.

A Song of Distant Earth

In uniqueness it dwells, in mystery it hides.

Old phantom of the opera playing to the stars,
Old sacred mountain filled with new eyes,
Old vestige city and ancient holy glow,
Old bearer of myths and spinner of tales,
Old popular culture that's invaded the sky,
Old star-bridge spider, old nest of abuse,
Old skein of roads for surface escapes,
Old seasons, weathers, geologies, and charm,
Old burial ground of humanism deep,
Cradle of nomads and hallowed landscapes,
First planetary noir, first legend unleashed,
Half composed by human art, depravity, and pride,
Defined by children's expectations of home,
Loved more in being lost, dreamt more in dying,
Embellished by memory and drowned in history.
And all this only hints of what you once were.

Did you welcome our departure?
Do you bask in aloneness,
Is your self-contemplation finally arrived?
Do you love us all the more
For this stellar abandonment,
For our vanished transgressions,
For the air now clean, the trees magnificent,
The oceans fluid and replenished once more?
How many wounds have you managed to heal?
Did we pray to you enough? Do I re-create you well?
Are your landscapes now made legitimate,
And do your tall tales once more speak?

How could you ever long for our return?
Are you not the victim of our every transgression?

Imperial planet, new House of Parliament,
One time soggy wet rag of a world,

Ice-caps melted, animals extinct.
We debated having to move you, steal you,
Insulate you, preserve you inside a silver globe,
A witch ball in the night, a prized trinket,
With memories projected on the inside screens,
Your histories displayed, your stories retold,
In a vast running playhouse for the stars.
Your locations live on,
Your recollections sustain,
Your places re-engender,
Your lives we retain.

And if, at some distant, galactic gathering,
A social event for the best of your children,
Someone casually mentions your name,
Brings back these thoughts of our common home
After so many vanished and forgotten years—

How will you be recalled?
Like Byron's lover...
With silence, and tears.

V. Riley's World

The Child

One year old...
With a topknot of hair like a sheaf or spray,
Big swollen cheeks and chubby double chin,
Her face so full of a clumsy wonder
That is still too young to be wary or precise.
In coveralls and "work shoes" she walks with a stagger
(Bump—down she goes, surprised at the floor),
Her gestures tentative, her brief cries small,
Her smile all sudden nubs of teeth.
Her tiny finger and sharp nail poke at my lips
As I hold her, feed her, her head on my arm,
As we alternate in fastening the bottle to her mouth.
And I—staring, lost in her face,
Drowning in a huge overwhelming love—
Can't move my eyes away from hers;
I'm locked in a fascination and joy—
I don't want to let go, don't want to abandon
What she is, the *now*;
Writing this is unbearable
For there's too much love—
As I walk and carry her, she clings to me,
Me, old barren self who feels
As shriveled as a flayed tree-trunk,
But who now has this life perched in his limbs,
This satchel of promise,
This delightful small self;
If tears weren't so miserably sad
I'd cry—or write, or sing—
Stupidly, foolishly,
And yet I do hum, quietly, softly,
Because lulling her to sleep
Is more important than poetry;
She is wonder enough as she is.

While I think of miracles,
Ecstasy and life,
She just sleeps...
She just lives.

The Dreams at the Bottom of the Sea

Where do our old discarded dreams go?

They're wrapped in stiff burlap, I imagine,
Tied to weighty bricks of reality
And tossed in the vast vault of the sea,
To plummet, stuffed tote-bags of longing,
To a dank and abysmal ocean floor
Where, now anchored, they hover and glide,
Toss like mummies, derelicts, squid,
In cold currents of blue algae-fog.

Where, you might wonder, do they talk, feel?
Touch? Commune? Spin old tales?
Share lamentations in their exile from light?
Do these black sporangia on dead sea-stalks,
In the bleak night-tides of that silent town,
Still dream on? Maintain secret hopes?

For—who knows?—someday
The slug of a sunken mer-child,
Repressed and punished yet eager to be born,
Will undo one knot, hold close one cord,
And slowly, gently, carefully, rise—
Following the buoyant and ugly old globe
Through flickering lights in organic murk,
Upward, ascending, embryonic, and free—

To the varied, the spawning,
Sun-shattered,
Sky.

Lullaby for Abby

(Composed to help
A certain child fall asleep)

Give a cheer,
Guess who's here,
Little Abby's in town.
We'll have fun,
Everyone,
Now that Abby's around.
Get to play
All the day
Till asleep we fall down.
We're so happy
Little Abby's
In town.

You're a treat,
Small and sweet,
We smile at the sound
Of your walk,
Of your talk.
"I precious," you sound.
At our lunches,
"Love you bunches!"
(Your line of renown)
Make us happy
Little Abby's
In town.

And each day that you come here
Brings a joy which is new.
There's a squirrel out the window—
You say "skirl!"
That's so you.

You're the one,
Like the sun,

Who brings light to the ground.
You say "sit"
(Where I can't fit).
What a treasure we found.
Just your name
Makes a game.
We love you profound.
We're so happy
Little Abby's
In town

All Things Simple

All things simple,
And all things kind,
Are often rejected
By the analytic mind.

If obvious and clear,
They're seen as being poor,
As if lacking complexity
Makes them lack more.

But I love things frank,
Ingenuous and true,
The common right solid,
And the standard, of you.

For if anything is absolute
Or sure in what I feel,
I have *you* to thank,
The certainty: you're real.

And so, the life you bring,
The life that you make mine,
Is absolutely simple,
And absolutely kind.

Abby At Three

We're not as often under the table
But drawing is now appealing again;
She can recognize her name,
And she wanted to know what a "spiral" was.

Abby days.

She still loves the "crystals."
We spill them on the floor and group them by type:
"Here are red ones—and green ones—
And *there's* a yellow cats-eye!"
She speaks in such crescendos of excitement.
Then her foot in the middle
Scrambles the symmetry.

With prisms we fling rainbows on the walls or ourselves,
Make her toes into glowing little toy crayons.
We blow bubbles and pester them,
Till they splatter against us in soapy-wet surprise.

Small sensory wonders.

When she's tired,
She withdraws behind sad whiny tears.
Everything is "No!" or "I don't want to!"
The universe seems wrong to her,
And you want to change it, knowing that you can't.

She loves "Nana's" ivory-lace dress.
A lady in appearance, she races unladylike
To seek hidden Riley,
And finding her she *screams* in absolute joy.
"Hide again!" she yells.

It's a common response:
I read her a book, she says "Read it again."
We watch a video, and "Let's watch it again."

Plus, she's in that "Why?" stage.
She takes every answer and makes it another question:
"What comes after fifteen?"
Sixteen, I say.
"Then what comes after sixteen?"

She leads me by my finger from room to room.
I'm a captivated captive.
She sits among pennies
And holds them between her toes.
I tell her, "Piggies bank."

All simple pleasures,
But uniquely cherished,
In moments so rich
And overwhelming, for me…

Wonderful days,

Abby at three.

Many Returns

When roads are just distance,
And time means good-bye,

When aloneness sits near
As I cross long nights,

Then befriending thoughts
Make my goal so true:

Arrival, a home,
And a face,
You.

The Everything Box

The best gift Abby ever received
Came in a small, plain, unwrapped box.

Her uncle gave it to her.
He said it was a gift especially for her,
Something she could hold on to forever.

But when he gave her the box,
He surprised her by saying,
"You *know* what's in here."

Abby wondered.
"Is it a small doll
With blue jacket and pink shoes?"
She had seen such a doll
In a store the other day.

"That's in there," her uncle said.
"And more."

She was curious now.
"Is there *another* doll in there,
A boy doll too? And a little toy dog?
And brother and sister dolls?"

"That's in there," her uncle said.
"And more."

But so many dolls would take up
All the room in the box.
She suggested something
Too large to fit in.
"Is there a dollhouse too,
With big windows,
And a Christmas tree in the living room,
Little newspapers by a chair,
Toy fruit in a bowl,

And a fence outside?"

"That's in there," her uncle said.
"And more."

Abby suggested items even larger.
"Is our house in there,
Our car, the front porch,
The trees in the yard and the hedges around it,
The lamp-post that doesn't work,
The other houses on the street,
Everyone who lives in them,
All my friends and their toys and their pets?"

"That's in there," her uncle said.
"And more."

Abby became even more insistent.
"Is the city in there, and the bridges beside it,
The river we cross, the buildings in town,
All the different people
And the boats on the water,
The taxi-cabs and buses,
The traffic lights, the candy store,
The bookstore, the *big* store with escalators,
Even the train-tracks where we put pennies?"

"That's in there," her uncle said.
"And more."

Abby let her thoughts go wild.
"Are animals in there, squirrels, birds,
The deer in the woods,
Clouds and rainbows—and even the rain?
Are there sports and swimming?
Is the beach in there,
With all of us walking up the sand-dunes together?
Are there oceans, and dreams,
All the things I *imagine*,
Princes and queens and castles and knights?

Everything I've seen, read about, heard,
The sun, the moon, the stars,
Other planets, galaxies,
And…and…"

"That's in there," her uncle said.
"And more."

Abby was exhausted.
She said, in desperation,
"I don't understand!
How could so much
Fit inside just that little box?"
Her uncle said, "Open it."

Abby lifted the lid.
And she saw…
Herself.
The box held only a small mirror.

Her uncle explained,
"All that you said came from you.
All you described—it's already *in you*."
He paused, then added,
"The best gift I can give you, Abby,
Is to remind you how much
You already have,
And just how much you already
Are."

Abby stared into the box.

"It's all in *me*?" she said.

Her uncle nodded,
And pointed at her forehead.
"It's in *there*," he said.…
"And more."

Abby looked pensive.

She stayed silent, for a moment.

But then she declared,
"No! You're wrong!
Not everything's in here.
Something I love very much
Is not here."

Her uncle looked shocked.
"What?" he cried.

Abby smiled,
And looked at him kindly,
And said:
"You."

For a long time after,
They argued, and laughed,
Over which one of them
Had really given

The *best* gift.

The Departed

I visit you often,
Joke with you, kid you,
Treat you as if
You're the girl next door,
Whose mother I just asked,
"Can Riley come out and play?"
We laugh, have fun,
Share small pleasures
And treats and joys,
Sometimes even longings,
Secrets and griefs,
But all on a level
And common open ground,
Where we're only similar,
Co-equals, travelers,
Friends in transit
At the train stations
Of life.

But then...

You leave the ground,
Gently rise from the earth,
You spread sudden wings
And take unexpected flight,
Hop aboard a gondola
That hangs down lightly
From a powered balloon,
With your freedom, intellect,
Charm, and grace in delicate tow.
You're transported away,
To rarefied realms where
I can only gaze at you,
Watch you in a telescope
As you pass before the moon,
On your way to an elsewhere
Which I, alas,

Can never reach,
Or touch.

And, as you vanish,
A spark in the luster
Of distant clear space,
You wave to me, kindly,
And say,
"Thank you!
Goodbye."

I am so in awe of you.

At Four

Socialization falls too soon.
"Butt-head" and "dumb-dork."
Is pre-school at fault?
"Let's play husband and wife:
You lie here beside me
And protect me all night."
Gender roles already!
"I can't sleep; I need *pills.*"
Where did she get that?
Suddenly she's a world not her own,
Made of media, input, culture's bad signs.
Her childhood's lost beneath the unreal.
Buried is the magic, the charm, the allure.
Woe and alas, they lose it at four.

But then, while we drove to the spaceport
And I asked why she was sad,
She moaned, "Because you're leaving."
I reached back, stretching my arm
So her tiny hand could hold my finger
All the way there.
Though her line at the gate,
"Have I told you today I love you?"
Was obviously learned, coaxed by Riley,
The small-armed hug was delightfully hers,
And so was her wave as I stared from above,
And the sorrow that pierced me
When they announced "time to board."
She still can defeat conformity's weight.

And so, in the future,
If ever weary or poor,
I yet will smile,
When I think of her at four.

The Obligation

What if…

We once inhabited
Some dark prior world
Where we sinned, did wrong,
Destroyed things precious,
Caused hurt, were cruel.

So that now, in *this* world,
We are led in secret
By latent recollections,
To atone, make well,
And this hidden support
Now forms the root
Of our drive, our longing,
To be kind, and to love.

For then there'd be logic
For this devastating need
That lurks, persuades,
That moves deep hearts,
Brings empathy to life,
Provides clear motive
For our one great dream—
The real, persistent,
If never understood—

To be *good* for someone.

Just to be good.

Abigail's "Yes" and Isabelle's "No"

Abby sees kids across the playground
And her face fills with a tender hope:
"Maybe they can be my friends," she says.
Her sensitivity makes one protective.
She once even asked me,
"Why do I cry so much?"

Isabelle, however, is more contrary,
Sometimes a near storm of protest:
With a fixed glare beneath slanted brows,
Her lips tightly squeezed in rejection,
Her soft grunts loudly imply,
She doesn't need anyone.

Abby longs for wonder, the "other,"
And a right clear world.
Isabelle wants her self-reliance proven.

Abigail says "yes" and Isabelle says "no."

Two words for the future,
Two means of exploration.
Wary optimist and tiny fighter.
Who has the advantage?
And why should a winner
Always have to be?

It's a shame I even think this,
When one is only five,
And one is only three.

To You, in That Other World

Did I imagine it well?
Did I bring your life justice?
Did you get what I hoped
Would be found, by you?
Did I make the names right?
Do you love the child I imagined?
Do you appreciate these quaint celebrations
Of her, and of that other child…and you?
Did I mark well their growing years?
How long should I imagine them?
How long *can* I?

And, concerning that other
Incarnation of myself
(Who I'd rather *not* imagine),
Are you as seamless for him,
As you were for me?
Are he and I that different?
How much are we the same?
Did his presence there surprise you?
Did you appreciate my subtle leading you to him?
Was his existence a satisfying revelation?
How went that first meeting?

I hope I've been accurate,
Though of course I'll never know.
Do I mimic his point of view
(As sometimes, I think, he invades mine)?
Did you enact the right moves,
Play the right tropes?
Are you now both archetype and actor?
(And, thus, a bit too much like me?)

I so wanted to be there,
Just to offer my blessings,
Though I would have stayed hidden,
Polite in shadows, off stage, silent.

The universe might have crashed, though,
On noticing my presence,
The contaminating lethal subject of myself.
As you'd say, in your way, joking, as usual,
"No universe can handle *two* Mykol Ranglens."
No. Indeed.

How goes that other Homeworld,
Is my fantasy of it real?
I've become a little frightened
Of forgetting all I knew of you,
All that happened between us.
Even these desperate poems might go.
When I finish this last one
(On this mostly created if "overheard" other life),
I'll be ready for a new and separate self.
I'll forsake these creations,
Maybe even publish them
As a means of disposing them,
In one more abandonment
Of what we hold dear,
Of our own small if significant
Children.

Maybe I should leave
This cold room where I write,
Meet other people,
Find some replacement,
As you, luckily (I presume),
Did for me.

You still remain a figure
In my narrowed landscape.
I want to ask you
To stay a bit longer,
But my universe apparently
Won't allow such things.

I should let this poem go.
I know you'll never see it.

(And yes, I knew that you snuck
Your quick peeks at my tentative lines.
I wish you still could.)

I *will* quit soon,
Let all this fade,
Cut losses, move on.
Cast away these jottings.
Let them float to some other
Downhearted soul.
Tomorrow, for sure.

I can even hear you grumbling,
Practical as always,
"There's little point
In hanging on."

Definitely tomorrow.

I will.
I promise.

VI. Dark Galaxy

Futures Past

Since the time I was born
The population of the Earth
Has tripled.

This frightens me.

And by the time I die,
Who knows what multiple—
Or fraction—will define
Its slow apocalypse then?

Do I really want to see that?

Once, as a young, star-eyed,
Science-fiction enthusiast,
I longed to know the future.

And I will.

I have.

But instead of
Feeling privileged,
I seem more

Condemned.

Night Thoughts

The universe is haunted,
Not by spirits, but by us.

Our ranging thoughts
Leak into space, crowd the stars,
Seep down onto planets
And stain them with our lives.

We populate the galaxy
With mind-spawn, apparitions,
Unleashed demons from imaginations in heat,
Products of obsessed and unfulfilled loves.

The sky's a black Rorschach slate,
The planets arenas, the stars players
In our simple and primitive mind's game.
We people even *people* with self-made selves,
Fulfilling our prophecies by making all things
Either good or evil, means or ends,
And then, generous, we set them free,
As if bestowing life is self-liberation.

Thus we seek, but we cannot find.
We've only let go in order to let be.
And we're left then, haunted,
In a universe that's haunted,
Where haunted people
Live haunted lives,
Where we search for others
But find only ourselves,
Too well known
And too over-defined,
We are all we'll ever get
To cherish or to watch.

The cosmos *is* bigger than our minds.

But, alas, not by much.

In the Morning of Galactic Creation

There, at dawn, in the Galaxy's first light,
One group said, "We believe in Space,"
And another group said, "We believe in Time."
And then they went to war.
Smoke obscured the morning thereafter.

Maybe they understood the comforts of extinction,
What happens to a race that knows it's dying
And yet can't believe in the changing of fate?
Did they feel like glaciers creeping to their ends
With iceberg slabs drifting into the future?
Could they control their latter-day destinies
By exporting lives, tooling new singularity selves
To establish desired Galactic conformity?

Where did they arrive? What worlds infiltrate?
What late terrors do we now inherit?
What has "inhabited" really come to mean?
Just how long is meant by "forever?"
And how did they think? What did they want?

If the Airafane believed in Space and thus feared Time,
They would seek a foundational universal structure,
Connection, slow change, stately control,
Custom, history, the marrow of moments,
The gradual melting into ceaseless Place.
Diplomats of loss, they'd grow free of weight,
"Majestic, elegiac, silent," like trees.
For in needing to hold all, they'd touch everything,
Demystify compliance, accept no difference
Between futures and pasts.

If the Moyocks believed in Time and thus feared Space,
They would hide from the universe in its radical corners.
They'd seek the intensity of every new present,
Become ruthless individualists, solitary, brutal,
Obsessed with clocks, with rise and fall,

With motion, fret, doom, possession,
Anxious brinkmanship pushed to the edge.
They'd dread isolation, become heavy with burdens,
"Restless, passionate, tragic," like humans,
Callous, resolute, hunters of the night.

Thus I see them, there in the dawn,
Squaring off, preening, overly proud,
Starting their galaxy-wide aggression,
Their centuries of bickering, pettiness, sneers,
Of marshaling death-rays and fleets of bombs,
Of tearing apart solar systems whole.

But did they have to saturate *all* known stars?
Direct *our* fortunes as well as theirs,
Bleed into planets, manipulate the chances
Of negotiating our own private darkness?
Make us ponder, with each new landfall:

"What mad underside of this planet beckons?
Why did we inherit the late terrors
Of these two dying races' primeval screams?
Why were we lied to?
Why did they trick us, hate us, condemn us?
Why did they toy with our wishes and lives?
Why help us, to destroy us?
Why dangle new worlds and then draw them away,
Hide behind equations, justify torture
By imposing cosmic 'laws'?
What's behind what they've done?

What's behind what *I've* done?"

Oh deadly and blue galactic dawn,
Swarming with radiation from young brute stars,
Though you witnessed two mighty races fall,
Will you someday reawaken, blaze a new light,
And shed on their legacy *any* light, at all?

The Dwelling Above the Clouds

At every story's end,
In this ghost-town obscure,
The house and its tenant
Are never certain, never sure.

It's sedate, if not splendid,
Quiet, if not serene,
Not a palace nor a fortress—
Turned in, seldom seen.

The woman who waits there
Neither dwells nor abides;
She is silent, she is chosen,
She is one with what she hides.

Absorbed and absorbing,
Ever weary, in her womb,
In her labyrinth of despond
And faithful narrow room.

She toys in that shelter,
Lives dreams, sheds lives,
Imagines till she's real,
Plays at lovers and at wives.

Clouds draw around her,
Bathe her dry in cold steam,
Where she plots her stellar booty
And tawdry clever schemes.

Enthroned in these vapors,
Hardly lost, over found,
Her serenity imprisons,
Her simplicity's unsound.

Oh, for the secret,
If once I only knew,

The sad dark story
That led to this you.

For there, at the end,
I might help, make you see,
That your house, though private,
Locks out a wide sea.

It's time now for new worlds,
To be open to new skies,
For clouds to uplift you,
And not shroud you in lies.

Come away then, loved friend,
My keeper of low flame.
Let's engender, ride together,
And bury sorrow's name.

We yet might have a chance,
Though I grant it's only slight,
As vague as the travel dreams
We follow each night.

For the ways you'll never be,
And the lives I can't command,
Still bind us, constrain us,
To your Mykol, and my Anne.

A World Called Little Redemption

The advertisement,
Stamped on a wall in a ruined city:

When the universe sours,
When pleasure wilts and excitement dies,
When your dreams forsake you,
When hope runs off with a forgotten enemy,
When you've outlived your past and lost your calling,
When you worship gods who abuse their followers,
When you want to be ruled strictly by desire,
When you follow authority that hates its disciples,
When you lose your standards but can't change your way,
When you long to abandon and leave your self behind
And yet still remain exactly what you've become—

Then gather your wondrous toys together,
The bright trinkets of post-terrestrial Earth,
And join the trickling but constant migration
That flows to this ironic, highly theatric,
And self-indulgent vain little world
Called, so rightly, *Little Redemption.*
It's a ghastly place, not for everyone.
But—you have to face it—
It might be for you.

The planet,
Approaching:

Like a stone flung at you,
A milky pearl cracked and blemished
With pink, yellow, and dingy brown.
You enter its atmosphere,
The sky turns violet like a cheap boudoir,
Then a bloody and unnatural pink.
You descend, you hurtle across the flats,
The shrub and stone and empty sand,
Like the Great South Desert you left behind,

Where humans squeeze into crowded cities
That seem out of place, like inflamed sores
In an ironed-out and oven-baked plain,
Like scabs or blisters pushed up through skin.

You near the city,
You reconnoiter, you probe:

Metal towers bristle forth
Like some impossible crystalline growth,
A microscopic view of a killer virus.
Garish colors make walkways glint
In hazardous webs to catch new victims.
Buildings rise like sharpened claws.
Lights produce a headache flicker
That seems to glare *beneath* your eyelids.

Two types of architecture prevail:
One monolithic, fascist, commanding,
Huge geometries that impose regularity,
Blocks etched or scarred with window-lines
Bright enough to glow even at day.
The second style is a jumbled graffiti
Gathered at the higher structures' base,
A mechanical neon plastic fungus
Resembling trash to be swept away,
As if this baroque excess and waste are calls to arms
Against the wealthy blocks behind.

The city beckons, and then it repels.
Then the repulsion itself *becomes* a beckoning.
You enter it in order to test its reality,
And you stay because it tests yours.

You enter the city:

Your senses are assaulted.
Pylons, piers, shingles
Of buildings rise above you,
Intricate with incredible display,

Striped balconies, spotted banners,
Big faces attractive and ugly,
3-D projections that run and stream
And vie for attention, glows that stab,
Moiré patterns in painful diffractions
Sliding across the flanks of towers.

The people resemble role-playing troupes:
Priests, tramps, courtesans, clowns,
Beggars, thieves, vagabonds, fools,
All in depraved overdone outfits:
Cloaks of metal chips, animal flesh,
Elaborate headdresses with armored machinery,
Mechanical boots with levers and rods,
Backpacks, chestpacks, wristpacks, shrouds,
Gowns of silk made of electric sparks,
Drapes of confetti, storm clouds, brass.

And over everything hangs a pall of shabbiness,
As if the circus is becoming bankrupt,
As if everyone knows it's on its last legs
Yet no one is willing to stop the fall.
The finery's unclean, the metal unpolished,
The banks of lights have conspicuous burn-outs,
The art's out of date, the faces droop,
The people drift indeterminately,
Throngs of emptiness filling up emptiness,
Their politics lost, their irony abandoned,
Their defeat abhorred as too outrageous.

You wince,
And hurry about your task:

You seek bureaus of imports and exports,
Customs, taxation, census data, property,
And you're told at all of them
That the information is classified,
That no *public* records exist.
(And you wonder if there are any records at all.)
You check libraries and information banks,
Electronic storage, filing services,

And you encounter only disorganization,
Classifications that make no sense.
You ask for help and people mock you.
"We can tell you about local history—
The Blood Plague, the Sunken Plains,
The Crystal Pillars, many other things,
But we keep no records about inhabitants,
Newcomers, visitors, even spies.
Here, information is not a commodity.
We respect people's chosen alienation."

You flee to the wastelands,
Where the wealthy war-games are played:

Imagine, first, an infinite mudflat.
Then quickly drain off all the liquid
Till gullies, cracks, and chasms appear.
Let the vast mud plain bake in the sun
And wait for a glaze to grow over everything,
A salt skin of drought and brittleness.
Allow stains of color to flow,
Dark caramel-brown dikes
That crawl like fingers across the ground,
Cruelly wrinkled rust-red ditches,
Large sulfur-yellow smears
Protruding in wrinkles from the dried earth.
But most of the desert leave pale,
A whitish-beige that fades into pink,
Tinged with bruise-like carmine and violet.
Then spread over everything a rosy sky,
Permitting its warmth to tint the land,
To sunburn the salt glaze,
To smolder in the hard shadows,
To raise odors of grit, dead plants, crushed glass.
Then stretch the scene for miles and miles—
Like the wide remains of a galactic flood,
A thick and deadly patterned muck
Hardened at the bottom of a cosmic barrel.

You see hox-cars,

The vehicles used in the war-games:

They're old refinished transport ships
That carry a stigma of guilt about them,
Because during the Blood Plague, years ago,
They were used to remove dead bodies
And dump them in the refuse of the Sunken Plains.
The planet's inhabitants get a weird pleasure
Out of advertising the shame of that time,
As if needing to remind themselves
Of just how dreadful events can become.
So instead of junking the old hox-cars,
They exaggerated their trappings instead,
Made them into derelicts or air-born slums,
Elaborate demonstrations of visual excess
In order to showcase the old despair.
Their roughly spindle blimp-like shapes
Were plated with patchwork and weathered armor,
With communication staffs dragging insect legs,
Till sides curved up in overlapping tiers,
Decorated with scarlet, beige, and bronze,
With red and black stripes like tribal masks,
Obscured by slats and modern gun turrets,
Foolish banners, long ribbons, obscene scrawls,
Blackened wounds or marks of decay,
A vast junkyard standing on end.

A war-gamer speaks,
Points at the landscape:

"It contains no life but itself is alive.
This land transforms,
The ground pushed up from pressure below,
Till fierce erosion cuts it away,
Sculpts it down in centuries of vast rise and fall,
The very bones of existence, the *truth*,
What the universe is really all about.

Off-worlders like you don't understand.
They believe a landscape is just a backdrop,

A barrier to be crossed, a blank to be filled.
But we lavish in it here. We *are* the landscape—
Timeless, dry, distilled, exposed.
We've stopped moving and proliferated into space.
We're new repositories of extravagant detail.
The indulgent excess of the cities
Reflects the massive formations of the desert.
We and the landscape are now the same,
Thriving on the heat and compression here.
We're squeezed out like some precious oil,
What's left after our pasts evaporate.
Look!—look there!—see those big salt patches?
They're residue smears of vanished lakes,
What remains after the rush and madness of rain,
The *survivors*, you see? The filtrated excess.
That's *us!* We were *made* for this place.
We bury ourselves in an entire planet.
We're painted players in a painted setting.
We *belong* here. This is our home."

And you, the founder, or creator,
Conclude:

It can't exist. But what if it did?
A refuge for the stars' lost and defeated,
A playground for all galactic outcasts,
For failed confessions and last temptations,
For abandoned actors with throwaway lives,
Who follow their singular disheartened path
To this legend of space, this tiny scarred world,
Where they, at last, can lose themselves,
In cities overdone with selfish flair,
In landscapes that brag a lack of deception.

A puny, loathed, scorned,
But *desired*,
World called Little Redemption.

The Sense of Wonder Passing

Can you feel it?
The sigh of longing
When you slowly realize
That something meant
To be always present
Is slipping away,
Departing quietly,
Taking its gradual
But recognized leave?

Old voices and promises—
They become lost,
Premonitions fade,
Memories turn into rumors,
SF becomes fantasy,
Outer space transforms
Into some new Dunsanian field
That we no longer, and cannot, know.
Old Earths are forgotten,
We become more aware
That even this realization,
That *this too*,
Shall likely pass.

Still, we imagine…
Lonely bars on lonely worlds
Under star-crowded but lonely skies,
Where spaceship crews relate their tales
Of the highly unlikely, and impossible to trace,
But ever evocative, Legends of Space.

Yet the mood of those legends is leaving now,
Taking with them the alien beacons
That wave beyond horizons at night,
The buried vaults and forbidden cities,
Signs of old wars, planets like cathedrals,
Gothic retreats in gloomy forests,

Deserted temples, carvings on cliffs,
Treasures protected by Flying Dutchmen
Or the ghosts of a drowned stellar Atlantis,
Relics in caves, hidden secrets,
Quiet planets that revolve discreetly
In starry and tenuous backdrop realms.
Where are the litanies of worlds now?

When a cherished sense of wonder fades,
Sorrow comes to you *without* a flourish.
It's not like the brutality of Mariner 4
When it discovered sudden craters on Mars
And swept away the years of imaginary canals,
Soft green life, bluish-pink hills, skating on ice,
And demolished us with its black-and-white
Sterility of an old, dead impoverished moon.

No, it's not that bad,
But 'tis enough, 'twill serve—
To take childhood away,
Forsake romance, let songs fade,
Weaken spells and sweep away mystery,
Corrupt grandeur, diminish the sublime,
Wave a pall of despair through the brain
Till anxiety builds an elusive dread,
A disturbing irrepressible fear
That something has left,
Gone amiss, gone wrong.

And then we find
That behind all our stories
A bleaker story lies,
The realization of a world
Beneath the world,
That it's not only dangerous
But ignoble, paltry, bland,
Depleted of marvels,
That it lacks the strata
Which cosmic archaeology
Once imbued with great wonders,

With so many dreams
Once our own.

The universe withdraws then,
Into private Deep Time,
And we, the rude tramps,
Know we've come too late,
That disconnected stories fall around us,
Like dulled coins in an emptied fountain.
And we can't read them.
They're in a foreign tongue
Which is too dark and cold
For its whispers to reach us.
We hear only the good-byes.

And feel only the longing,

Longing for what was
For what evades us,
For what we once were.

The longing.
The longing.

Atom Style

An Art Deco clear-line assurance
That comes with snarky optimism too,
As if clean design can save the universe
And sparse decoration remake us all.
The men—square shoulders, fedoras, wide pants,
The women—tilted hats, long skirts, bare arms,
Are deeply etched in this given scenario
And almost hide the noir roots beneath.

Its city is mundane and cosmic at once,
An old-fashioned future with smooth polished glitz,
Whose not-so-subtle upbeat tone can almost offend.
For hiding behind its jukebox skyline
Is the radioactive taint of the nuclear desert
And the unresolved sexual politics from years of war.
Even its cherished celebrated austerity
Distracts from its myriad social biases.
The belief that the future is ultimately attractive
Can lead instead to restricted visions, based on fear.
Its finned topless display-cars lack friction,
And when they stop for blondes in wide hats,
The driver's eye squints, his thin mustache grins,
And standardized gendered theatrics unwind.

The city's denizens are mired in bigotry,
Even if they *are* neatly cleansed and sterilized.
They're spawned by the hidden generator in our minds
Which, alas, makes everything possible,
And everything also seen before...at least once.

The Airafane too preached a modernist dynamic,
But let's not forget where *they* ended up.

The Woman Who Spoke For the Sea

I am all ports of call,
All islands in the stream,
All hidden blue grottos
And bright sunken dreams.

My arms are made of water,
My caress laced with foam.
I am visitor and traveler,
Always moving, always home.

Shorelines define me
But borders I despise.
Amorphous I remain,
In abundance I thrive.

Transcending hard earth,
Fluid spirit of fluid space,
I come, then I go,
And I leave little trace.

The ocean is a transient,
Immortal, on its own,
Promise given, promise taken,
All you've wanted, all you've known.

Seek for me in silence,
In the calm, or in the storm,
Beside bonfires on coastlines,
Or in candle flames torn.

And feel no regret then,
No longing for what you lost;
You did well having had me,
At no sacrifice, no cost.

I promise to be generous,
Yet I'll stay self-contained.
I've held you, even loved you,
But my *soul*, I retain.

Earth, Cheap

For sale, used planet, a fixer-upper's dream.
Internal combustion engine still working,
Though exhaust and cooling need some repair.
New widespread paint job not required,
But a light rub-down in places might help,
Just to smooth off any barnacles or crust
Left by the negligent previous owners.
The air conditioning might seem old-fashioned,
But those ancient volcanoes have nostalgic appeal,
And they require no recharge or fancy batteries.
In the ruins a quaint zombie infection might reside,
Creating inevitable upholstery stains,
And past dwellers have left many ghosts,
But these can become great tourist attractions,
And provide memorable campfire tales
For those renewing the beaches and forests,
Which, of course, will need to be addressed.
The oceans' colors might look faded from space
But they're easily restorable, in time.
Alignment and steering could be slightly off,
But not hard to correct, and the present orbit
Involves no dangerous upcoming traffic.
Finally, the price—only 2×10^8 standard,
Which is *very* good for today's market.

Naturally, no credit can be accepted,
Not in our current inflationary universe.
But trade-ins are welcomed,
Especially small main-sequence stars,
And we'll consider even asteroids and moons.

Willing to negotiate!

Crashing Suns

Let us go then, block-jawed star trooper,
And conquer the still yet unknown universe,
Take our popular culture to the stars,
Justify all bright futures in space
With unreliable narratives from distant pasts.

Airafane City,
Art Deco towers with elevated walkways
Bright in the heat-lamp of galactic dawn,
Where deadly unleashed synchrotron radiation
Was followed by invasions, earthquakes, plagues.
So many lost causes, so many falling skies,
Disasters in panel-stacks or triptych displays,
Worlds ending luridly in four-colored doom.

The Airafane woman and mighty Moyock man
Decided in their high-stakes world-spinning roulette
That, as many have conjectured besides me,
"You'll take time and we'll take space."
But crazed animosity and pleasant affability
Weighed out mutual long-term destiny,
(Ours too, the whole galaxy's),
And they agreed to meet a billion years hence
To tally notes and count dead bodies,
To end their game of endless endgame,
Mete out winnings of mother-ships, planets, dead old stars,
After which both groups could welcome second lives.

But what about *our* lives? Second, or first?

Crashing suns and forbidden moons,
Orbiting jets and solaristic queens—
Shored-up images against our decline,
Against the certain death of human imagination.
I saw the black empress in Griffith Observatory,
I saw the silver queen as deposed suzerain,
I saw the loved adventurer against her green sky,

I saw the blond hero pursuing, finally, the right woman.
But I wanted her to run a spaceship factory
And not be servile worshipping flunky,
I wanted daughters to become rogue scientists,
I wanted the queen to kick her lying fiancé's ass,
And I admired the women who stood beside
The winged man, the ringed man,
The rocket man, the lightning man.
They were wonderful. They deserved their release.
But it took the fall of many civilizations
To fulfill any promises, even *after* that fall.

Pinto Vortando and Pia Folinari—
Names like that will help you survive
Any protracted stellar Long Night.

Moyock Mountain was filled with mouths,
Intake valves for our turgid visions,
Swallowing human imaginary thoughts.
The mountain didn't require normal sustenance
Since our brains became its standard fare.
But why are *we* always the galactic victims?
Who are we, anyway?
Why is every alien in the universe after us?
What's so special about human-made goods,
Our copper deposits, our city parks, our fast cars,
Our insurance policies and B-rated histories?
Why do stellar vampires crave *our* blood?
Who died and made us so goddamned important?

Is popular fiction the new epic of our time?

Airafane City,
Flying saucers over chopped-up buildings,
Derricks and forklifts reaching down from above,
Waters rushing into the streets, frogs invading,
Colored ray-blasts seen even in the daylight,
Chromium Chrysler Buildings with holes,
Aliens tearing up suburbs built by Frank Lloyd Wright,
Snipers competing to become armies of the future,

And stand-up belligerents harping about terrors:

"I am destruction, I am the storm,
I bring revelation of what lies hid.
Your world's unlikely, your time is false,
My new perspective comes dark from within.
You're alone and frightened, tormented, un-free.
Your life and your planet are suspect, my friend.
To this chaos, this blight, you have no key."

I saw that passage in a notebook once.
I even think I know who wrote it.
But what does it matter?
Who do we save? Who might save us?
What nightmares have we alone unleashed?
Who gets tossed into the vacuum now
To cover our losses and lighten the spacecraft?
Why are the only ships that function well
Always the slave-ships?
And which SF futures
Will *we* pursue to hide in,
Justified, at last?

Here lies tragedy,
Once buried under comedy.
They tried to be compatible
But achieved only irony.

Here lies wisdom,
Once brought to you by intelligence,
But the sponsor in its vanity
Dropped empathy for malevolence.

Here lies God,
Was he Superman or loafer?
Nietzsche made him Batman
But he was really the Joker.

And here lies death.
Oh, how I wish!

But it still rules life,
Big sharks, small fish.

It's annoying, alarming,
Sad, and perverse,
To learn one lives
In a suspect universe.

I reinforce these memories
To offset the predicted
Collapse of our galaxy.
(The second collapse, I mean.
We missed the first one.)

And still, I ask again,
Where are *we* in all this?
Or have we now *become* "all this"?
Has the universe shut down already?
Lost strength, become subverted,
Permeated, corrupted, and then polluted
By some *other* creeping universe,
To make all these worries just latter-day
Epilogue, denouement, post-mortem,
Writing as autopsy, poetry as last breath?
Have we all been invaded already?

Airafane City,
Are you the galaxy now?
Do you sew up the night
With your spider-web schemes?
Do your transport roads cross dark space,
Your light-wire connections spin through
The future and parsecs both?
Is this the last blend of time and space,
Of quantum mechanics and general relativity?
Do you now *choose* the probabilities
Of the Schrödinger equation?
Or impose a Bayesian interpretation instead?
Run new variations of the double-slit experiment,
Create a multiverse from quantum foam,

And, for that matter, now that I think of it,
Do you see yourselves as particles or waves?
How do you interfere with yourself,
And how close do we have to get to you
Before we influence *your* experiments?

Is this the only way our world ends?
In ignorance, impunity, and in never knowing why?
As the millennia of rock-layers build,
As we define more geological eras
To show what we've done, on Earth, in space,
On every world we've come to inhabit,
Spreading our various anthropocenes
Across an undefined sterile galaxy,
Is this what you trained us for?
Are we fulfilling your best-laid plans,
Carrying on your bequest?
Just how connected to you are we?
Where do we come from,
Where did *you* come from?
And why must you take interest
In us at all?

I land on new planets
That I know once were yours
And I can't help feeling
A monstrous paranoia.

Airafane City,
Are you also just eruptions
From a crack in the earth,
An atom style, a noir punk,
A legend of space, a dangerous color,
One among many crystals and lights,
A child, an obligation, a sacred mountain,
A secret, a frame, a deception, a lie,

Or the very first of all first lights?

What the Coyote Said

You are destruction,
Your defenses grow lean,
Your secret's almost known,
You are not what you seem.

Though other stories end,
Your "Deep Story" thrives,
A suspended revelation
Told in Galaxy Time.

Expect new problems,
And a special new face,
Dangerous orbits,
Or Contested Space.

History might disown you,
A faction want you dead.
But you'll learn to control
All the darkness you've led.

Still, I wouldn't be you.
Your universe lacks pride.
It won't change if you tumble,
And won't care if you died.

But there's little to understand
In these musings I give.
They're only meant, in *my* way,
To encourage you to live.

So, do forget me.
What I mean, I seldom say.
I'm not even sure
I talk to *this* you anyway.

And you don't need *me*
To question all you've known,

You tease yourself enough
In these lines of your own.

So…carry on.
I've nothing more to say,
And you might thank your gods
You now cast me away.

Serious Remembrance

Outer space made us basic again.
We've entered the *post* post-human world.
We're breeders once more, made simple and real,
Primitives in Airafane mobile caves,
Crossing a stellar wilderness bright—if often dark—
Reduced to civilization that's retrograde and crude.

We've always had the purpose
Of racial survival, human preservation,
Old evolution's compulsive directive.
But maybe it's not needed anymore.
Survival isn't everything.
Animals and microbes might do better.
Even helping others is basically self-serving,
And spreading through the universe
Is less exploration than it is exploitation.
Maybe the galaxy is better off empty.
If we fill it, won't we just stagnate ourselves,
Kill anything new, take away inspiration?

I don't know where I stand in all this.
I want to think less, yet I'm too academic.
I can't help my removed perspective.
By trying to live, I leave myself behind—
And yet, with Clips, don't we all do that?
But we still can't help wanting to be ourselves,
Stand more apart, reject the new communication web,
The node-like implants in the uniform net,
Not wanting to be circuits in larger complexities,
A medium for media, a depot for information.

So, in order to become free, I can't be myself.
Should we abandon intellect? Retreat, go back?
Or become like the Airafane (whatever that means).
Give up their gifts and abandon curiosity?
But I want to know what's *behind* the gift—
I never wanted to be the person in charge,

But I did want to be the person
Behind the person in charge.

So planetary memory now goes cosmic.
Remembrance gains a forward look.
"Geological" becomes "technological,"
And cultural recollections are no longer Earthbound.
Before, we imagined Space. Now, it's Earth.

We long for the local *and* the universal,
Both the human and the non-human,
Environments of significance, models of scope,
Every world now made into a homeworld,
A remembrance of everything we have been,
And, emphatically, of what we might be.
But in gaining interstellar human freedom
We've de-centered nothing,
We've made *everything* a center.
We no longer inhabit an inorganic world,
We exist in a fully human-made world,
We're so much a part of it we can't extricate ourselves.
It's impossible to be an individual anymore.

And thus we only *remember* what Earth was like—
Alone, separate, pristine, unique—what it once seemed
Before we melted it down and painted the skies with it,
Made each planet into a station, a neuron, a transient,
Turned all specifics into pins inside a matrix,
Significant, but contained in some larger network,
Everything made primary because nothing is secondary,
And memory now is forever associated
With a new and uniform galactic anxiety.

In the future, each one of us
Will create a new universe.

But nothing will change.

Answers

And for those,
Only touch.

As I watched disasters
Falling through air,
A child lay
On my knee,
And I touched
Her infinite softness
Of hair.

I distrust "answers."

My hand on her head
Speaks more love
And care.

What you hold,
Believe.

We watch disasters.
But I touch
Her infinite softness
Of hair.

VII. Sanctuary

The Secret Identity

Not Clark Kent, nor Superman neither,
But a latent dark man-bat of the soul,
Flying by radar's insubstantial pulse
And groping, desperate, seeking in code
Beyond all longing, but hinting,
Reminding, that at the center of self
Is this other *secret* self,
This mysterious, mutated, darkened bird,
This tiny storm of determined desire
That must reach without hands,
See without eyes, fly alone,
Apart, withdrawn,
To endure....

And I remember, when young, awaking at night
And staring through empty windows of darkness
And thinking—in silent frustrated need,
As if losing the end of some wondrous dream—
"I want—"
Or more often, "I love—"
But not knowing where, or why, or *what*!
Just filled with a wild unguided affection,
A haunted craving or furious surmise,
And I'd think of Bruce Wayne
And the flying rodent that smashed his window
And told him, showed him, *his* secret self:
"You're Batman, my friend. I'm in you forever!"
And I, a pessimist even when young,
Wondered if someday, somehow—just maybe—
I too would be able to name this longing,
Bring home this fleet unknown fury,
This embracing-without-sight,
This wildness, this need.

And thus, now, after long years,
As I hear bat-squeals
Echo along roofs and walls outside,

As they speak to me in ciphers
And fragments from the dark,
In the fugitive screams
And whispers of sight,
I realize—I *know*—
The secret of identity
That to our window night brings…
Our longing is blind,
But our longing has wings.

The Birthday Moon

He dropped the moon into her lap one day
Because he, adoring, thought anti-gravity
An appropriate surprise birthday gift
For even *her* volatile irrational moods.
Forgive him, a mere scientist-apprentice,
And still so young that he loved completely.
Though she beamed at his gesture, moony, struck,
She then kicked him, furious—with hearts in her eyes.
His folly, her temper: such foolishness has charm,
Their untutored ineptitude guileless and true,
Full of love, if not tact, delightfully human.
In slops of emotion are our sole means to touch.
    So be thankful for love, its glory, our faults.
    We're all just children in auditions to be adults.

The Man Who Loved Alien Landscapes

He's no planet himself, no rock of safe repose.
He's more like an empty derelict in space,
Gliding before a star-infested night,
An alienated activist who tries not to be bitter,
Though he *did* say once, much too hastily,
"Landscapes are more important than people."

He doesn't know if he's socially in exile
Or simply withdrawn and self-isolated.
He's shocked he has a conscience.
His relationships are strictly one-on-one,
Constricted, contained, and very short-lived,
But he dreams of fervent and powerful longing,
An incendiary heart that lives on heat.

He thinks he "needs a mission,"
But he rejects most that are offered to him.
First-person narration he usually avoids.
He dreams of Ghost Worlds in a haunted universe.
He seeks caged flowers, spin vectors,
Lattice vanes, barrier gates to illusion jewels,
Caves, maelstroms, oceans with lids.
When he's too much into self
He yearns to dissolve and be lost in landscape,
In *alien* landscapes, unbearably new.

He fills his homes with captured demons
While opening to quickly replaced lovers.
He resides in many houses, builds new romances
From the remnants of his past and pieces of "you."
Space should terrify him but he loves new worlds.
He says, "I've built butterflies, even while destroying
Many a universe." It's one of his few cheap lies.
He talks as if he's encountered time warps,
Different eras, and continual creation.

He doesn't understand the potentialities of guilt.

Albert Wendland 183

His heart lives in winter, surfing on avalanches of change.
He knows he masters only interpretations,
Not objects, not things, and no renovations.
He seeks Affected Earths, realities gone wild,
Abstractions he can know while building his ideal,
His Gray Lord's identity behind a Black Knight.
His ships are all plague ships.
He fears he'll someday be approached and told,
"I'm not the *only* enemy you have."

His father, a rationalist, was a drinker but never drunk;
He had moments of profound if defeated wisdom
Above his implacable unfeeling stubbornness.
His mother, too sensitive, was terrified of life,
An artist without training, a desperate manipulator
Though everyone adored her. She lived in fear.
He inherited the best, and worst, of both.

He dreams of flying saucers half buried in icefields,
Disappearing spaceships in the Galactic Reach,
Crew-members vanishing on empty foreign planets,
Twisted trees that dance, huge glass coins,
Emerald icebergs, red-black volcanoes,
Lyres singing in snow-buried mountains.

He doesn't feel he's aging and maybe he's not.
He's seen so many worlds that times become space.
He lives in forgetfulness, but he knows he's afflicted
By secrets he can't reach, by a past he'd discard.
He's seen "the other side." He's seen more than several.
He'd rather see no more but he can't refuse.

He's solitary, stoic, withdrawn, alone.
His attachments unravel, become fugitive and uncontrolled.
He perpetuates the riddle that *he's* the one abandoned.
He's scared he'll never have what's so widely claimed,
A harbor, an anchor, a solace, a home.

When he writes, he stands on the edge of a precipice,
Scared of falling into a cauldron of emotions,

And yet wanting to do so, like skating on a ridge
While looking over, down, frightened of vertigo.

He's bombed out by the universe,
Stunned by recollections of color-coded worlds:
A brown desert beneath a pink sky,
A green sky over yellow-orange plains.
He nestles in colored and parti-striped cliffs.
That last is Homeworld—no surprise, of course,
Hardly even imagined.

He feels he's stalked by glows on the horizon,
Gleams in forests, hidden lamps, moonstruck trees,
Stars hanging from limbs like ornaments.
His worlds always have surprising artifacts,
Fleeting luminescence, furtive new life.

He avoids well-known historical exoticism,
The dreamy steam-heat glaze of centuries,
Recognized desires, glamorous Orients,
The West's narrative of ancient "lost worlds."
Starbound colonies he knows are compromised,
Disguised South Americas, distance that's false.

He seeks new reality that's hard as a diamond,
Stark alienation that's plain, direct,
But he knows he's surrounded by guarded dreams,
Where plantlife's colors run and bleed,
Where filtered tints never quite overlap,
Where perspective's disorganized, geology a challenge,
And new templates, new rules, new blanks must be filled.

Though he wants the universe and people both,
When he's with others he longs to be away,
And after seeing the sublime, he feels alone, even selfish,
In need of humble equality with a companion.
He does not choose his Romantic isolation,
He's no Byron, vampire, tormented loner.
He longs to love everything—then be madly in love
With only *one* thing, to the limits of his restraint.

He doesn't know where to place his cool objectivity;
It's too removed for galaxies but too intense for people.
And his need for touch, sensuality, contact,
Is both a celebration and a self-revelation.
He leaves behind both lovers and landscapes
As if attempting to shed his own old skins.

He doesn't lie to other people,
But he does to himself.

Instead of "flying" he wants to flow into space,
Be absorbed, lose the planet and *become* the sky instead,
Avoid Earth's distinctions, boundaries, maps,
Be both artist and canvas at once.

He forever ponders his own true role,
He's no skilled manager of impossible escapes,
And he always concludes, as if in desperation,
He's just a lone lover of alien landscapes.

Anglos Aweigh

Ah, the Anglo-Saxons, alliterates all,
Taught me a truism ten talents tall.
When I needed to be negative, they nudged me right,
By hinting "alliteration will harm her only slight."
So I declared (of her writing), "it's dry, almost drear,"
That I expected elation from her oft-easy cheer.
I then coupled this with compliments, cuddly and kind,
Of her usually upbeat and euphoric line,
Called her "master of motivation" (though "mistress" had more taste),
And "Queen of not-quitting," and "princess of post-haste,"
Even "guru and glory of all get-up-and-go."
I then stuck on a happy-face to soften any woe,
To convince her my pedantics were play, not spleen,
For I only meant to mentor and not to be mean.
And so, in reassurance, I respectfully remind you—
For Beowulf's boasts, and critiques of brevity,
A little *alliteration* allows a levity.

Nomads In Love

Sites passed,
Travelers' ways,
Temporary planets for transitory days.

Now at dusk arise shades new.
This last pale splendor
Is the color of you.

Solemn, quiet,
The field where she lay.
A gray sky, for a green day.

Countries wild can she unlock,
My lady of water,
My lady of rock.

Gems moon-white, dress dark blue.
It's Romantic twilight,
Or the landscape of you.

Remember that mist of thin small rain?
It's a hard kiss of memory,
Or a soft kiss of pain.

I'd trade home's peace, yes, to be sure,
For such moveable locations
With you, once more.

Riders of time, anchors in flight,
We're known to hold hands
Even during our goodnights.

And when we found each other,
You didn't need my name.
You simply called, and I simply came.

The Necessity of Human Weakness

We need it for sympathy,
We living that are flawed,
For our knowledge after failure
And the understanding heart,
Because, in the end, we *all* slip.
Our strength's not in triumph
But in the wisdom of regret.

Without frailty there'd be no art,
No awe, joy, longing, and youth,
No poignancy, poetry,
Attraction of opposites,
Jury by peers,
Dangerous roses,
Dreams, compassion,
And especially…
Love.

In Praise of Travel

The days swell with input.
Experience grows
As wide as the land.
It seeps into our minds
With mysterious invasions:
"What happened that day?"
Hallucinations, or moods?

We discard small-mindedness,
Keep quarrels indoors,
Choose to be silent
In order to relish
And not roughly gulp
The magnificent grandeur
That haunts us each day.

No binding destinations
Mar such a trip.
Reception is compressed,
Fierce and raw.
We grow whole, we abide,
And what we behold
We want to become.

We're freed of alibis.
No false comforts
Hide our desire.
For once we're replete,
And each day's longing
Is stirred by each night.
Lands beckon.

Softly we murmur,
"This is what Life
Is supposed to be."
Then, near frightened
That Life might respond,
We silently proceed.
We gently travel on.

If I Should Forget Thee

If I should forget thee,
In fades of old age,
If the mind should fester
With roadblocks and haze,

Then be sure that you show me
More than once your loved face.
Its memory I might lose,
But its outline I'll still trace.

If I seem all mired
In directions gone obscure,
Take my silence for fulfillment,
And grieve me no more.

Though my joys might be simple,
Think not they'll be less.
If I laugh when you kiss me,
It's from pleasure, not jest.

And feel little sadness
If your words don't get through.
I'll not be disturbed,
If I know they're from you.

And, when all else fails
(As I'm sure all else will),
When perception founders
And the heart's almost still,

When there in my labyrinth
Of nostalgia and regret,
I still seem empty,
Entangled and upset,

Then patiently, softly,
(It might take several times),
With clarity, with kindness,
Read me these lines.

The Chariot of Sparrows

The banshee came in a black death coach
And flew soot victims to cold earth realms.
Charon's ship plowed waters of ink
To lay dead sailors on lost dead shores.
Angels flew their meek pale spirits
To equally pale villas in clouds,
Where boredom, laced with finery and gold,
Softened one's edge in rounds of flat joy.

Yet, if this ultimate choice were mine,
I'd prefer Aphrodite's team:
The chariot of sparrows.
To take me to insubstantial lands
Where substantial longings make ghosts that crave,
Where figures desire but are carved in glass,
Where ecstasy's on hold in static tableaus,
And life's made perfect in lifelessness supreme.

Yes, take this late warm spirit of mine
And draw me like a meteor across dead skies,
Lift me from serene conceptual space
To follow emotion's hard-wrought line,
Plant me with majestic reminders of love,
With symbols and icons worshipped in private
By poets and prophets afflicted with delight.
Take me in sorrow. Take me in flight.
But take me yet longing into *my* good night.

Ghost Hordes

There are nights I feel
I'll meet myself one day,
Some alternate Ranglen
From an ulterior reality,
From a singular realm
In a plural Omniverse
(Ultraverse? Magnaverse?).

We might explode on contact,
A collision between anti-matter and matter,
Creating a newly personal black hole.
Or maybe we'll become pals,
Break out cigars, trade opinions,
Raise exaggerated mirrored eyebrows
At shared secrets for secret-sharers,
Subtle in-jokes, one-sided conversations;
They'd be both fascinating and boring,
Since we'll already know what'll be said.

I remind myself
That physics can't allow it,
But I think our universe
Has given up on physics.
"It's so last millennium."
Light-space, time-space,
They're metaphors in the end.
Even literary realism
Surrendered to flexible
Post post-realities long ago.

I almost feel it's already happened,
That once before I met
Some figment of my self,
A cocky subterranean other,
A released metaphysic
Shaped like a coyote
With a voice of foreboding.

I insisted, "I know you,"
Though I really did not.
I was too full of bravado,
Countering with taunts
When I only wanted words,
His secrets, his travels,
A full list of his loves.
I wanted to know if they
Were different from mine,
Or where to find them.

All these speculations arise
From feelings I've encountered lately.
Parts of my past I no longer recall,
Encounters once apparently drastic
But now more like emancipated selves,
Scattered into winds, chasing after partners,
Friends, acquaintances, shared affiliates
That I once found in trees.

They brew and simmer
In my turgid mental depths
Where I labor to parse them.
"Was I there? Did I do that?"
I grasp at minnows
That slither and flee.
And do these other selves
Also grapple with a stalking
Demolition of scrutiny?
This progressive decay?
Do they ask, like me,
Just how much excavation
Can one brain take?

I feel that, someday,
I'll become overwhelmed
By this vast line of selves
That seek me, follow me,
Like refugees from past mishaps,
Hordes of the abandoned and neglected,

Dark streams of fugitives on plains,
Hazarding forward in search
Of their victim,
Their father, their child.

I long for them
While also wanting
To push them away,
Learn all they know
While remaining free,
Escape their
Life-determining
Mistakes.

I imagine them in widescreen gothic baroque,
Treading under clouds of savage gods
That drip ink from roiling skies,
Like victims of a grand stellar disaster,
Carrying pikes with severed goats' heads,
Holy pilgrims or seekers of prey,
Acolytes of illusions, of all my premonitions
In forced lock-step of regrets, intrigues,
The secrets inside me not fully known,
The lives unfathomed, riddles en masse,
The pasts and parts, all the roads not taken,
Bearing down on me like the feeble undead,
Here to proclaim, "You're in danger,"
Or to prove finally that I'm not myself,
To obliterate my solitude, expose deceptions,
Bury me beneath their undiscovered countries.
Hosts, armies, legions of the plain.
Or they come on floating barges
From unseen headwaters
Bearing torches at night.
They come in any great way
I imagine,
In any way they can.

And I welcome them, I await them.
As they converge around me

I want to hear their stories,
Want to know why my outlooks
Mean more than what they should,
Why I see in those I love
Other planets, other realms—
Why I love at *all*
When I believe I should be solitary,
What things I desire
When I disappear into space.

I even know a lot of them—
The man who married Riley
And fathered her children,
The man who loved Mylia
On her world of adventure,
The sullen yet competent spaceship pilot,
The scholar of popular cultures past,
The prisoner, the rebel, the nomad, the fool.
And the one who never speaks,
The one who hides and seldom moves,
The central character of my own Deep Story,
The figure I'm not sure I *really* want to know.

So come to me, all of you,
From the plains, from the rivers,
From comets throughout the sky,
Come as brothers, come as sisters,
As potential correlations in unknown caves,
As vagabond hordes throughout the night,
Come in loneliness,
Come in solitude,
And at last,
Come in *triumph…*

To the nexus,
To me.

A Confession

Once, I considered
Writing a children's book,
In which a kind uncle
Asks a loved child,
"What's the *nicest* word
You can think of?"

She'd suggest possibilities:
"Candy," "play," "friends."
He'd say no.
"Home," "pets," "family."
Still, no.
"Trees," "the sea," "the stars."
Not close.

She'd beg to be enlightened.

He'd claim that her knowing
The word should be easy,
That it covers everything,
Applies to each person,
Event, possibility.

"Tell me!" she'd insist.

And he'd say,
As if obvious,
"The nicest word
In the language…
Is 'you.'"

…

And thus,
All in all,
To be sure,
To be true,

Each poem
I ever wrote
Was the poem
Of you.

A Temporary Planet for a Transitory Day

Spaceships over fields of twilight and snow,
Colored flames in flight above cold white down,
Beacons, portholes, rider-beams, and flares,
Green sparks of meteors, blue dots, red specks,
Prowling lights on missions, meetings, pursuits,
Loves.

It's a land of old memories,
Thoughts in animated dance on my desk.
The window's cold air slides icily down
And hits me sitting in my empty room,
Dark with its single hooded lamp,
Where I dream and welcome
Scenes from locations stirring in my past,
White nostalgia on a gray crystal day,
Cherished pictures rumbling up inside me
As if the mind too can growl when empty.

All because the weather's out-of-joint, crossed:
A December in October without November in between.
Comes sudden cold, and early snow powders
The yellow, brown, and crackling red leaves,
Encrusting the limbs, icing the earth—
Calling up memories of stellar exploration,
Adventures in outer space, tales of other planets,
Alien landscapes both imagined and real,
My adolescent friends in deep sweet dreams
Of uncharted, unfamiliar, unknown new worlds,
Where the seasons can color even high night stars.

Oh what wondrous settings I imagined,
Many of which I soon got to see and visit,
In spaceships like narrow Christmas trees in flight,
Or sleek cathedrals with stained-glass comp-screens,
Pursuing indefinite and far-off landscapes—
Iced lakes, jeweled trees, aurora-topped hills,
Where the open airlock's glow behind

Flung out my shadow to meet mysteries new,
Longings, secrets, sagas…come alive.

Like that one strange and quietly persistent
Craving, and suspense, for a sometime imagined
Black-haired woman in long winter coat,
In boots and high fur-lined collar,
Lean, independent, eager, and brave,
Standing by her idling dim-lit aircar,
Framed by resolve, excitement, desire,
Her skin chilled but warmed with yearning,
Her pensive lashes entangled with snow,
Her eyes and hair as black as the night
Between the shining and falling flakes.
She'd look up, till her eyes brimmed with stars,
Wet snowdrops pooled on her crescent lips,
On the moist delicate shells of her lips.

And I, in my room—or spaceship, whatever—
Lean back in my padded control-room chair
To recall these sights from a past long ago
 (While the glows from luminous switches
Glide pastel-prints on my hands and face).
I pause from my writing, enchanted by innocence.
And, while musing, almost smiling, I lift to my mouth
My emptied coffee-mug with its wide rim,
Not noticing yet that the coffee is gone…
And I feel its warmth, its pressure on my lips…
And…suddenly—
I'm reminded of *her* lips, *their* touch, moist,
From a woman I know now was incredibly *real*,
Who's suddenly *remembered* and not imagined,
Who was—God, yes!—that black-haired woman
From a cold other world in winter's dark night—
And I realize…it happened!
That planet existed, it's no longer misplaced,
And for once this yearning, this dream, was true—
In a wonderful if brief and fragile moment,
This she, and *that* she, are the same, are one.

I sit there astounded, in a humble deep awe.

The visions tumble, the memories meld,
The imagined long ago and this real recent past
Mingle, dance, interact, take form—
And I'm with her again, I recall the starlight
Defining the subtle contours of her face,
The gleams in her eyes like pearl-glints,
Like stellar reflections in ebony seas…
The sky, the aurora, the flakes of soft snow.

I marvel, I luxuriate, I lavish
In reclaiming her reality once more…

And I begin to write,
And for once I know
Exactly
What I will say:

"…I alone get to notice
That the flakes falling there,
Make white constellations,
In her midnight hair."

Author's Note

Though the poems in this collection stand on their own, since they're "written" by the protagonist of my two previous novels, you can gain a deeper understanding of them by examining *In a Suspect Universe* (where you'll find Mylia, Riley, and the planet Alchera), and *The Man Who Loved Alien Landscapes* (which contains Mileen, and more speculation about the Airafane and Moyocks). Neither book is essential for enjoying these poems, but they do add to the experience, and the poems, in turn, enrich the reading of the other two works. Also included here are loose associations with at least two more Ranglen novels yet to be written (*Contested Space* and *Galaxy Time*). As the Airafane apparently believed, and modern physics would love to demonstrate, everything connects.

Acknowledgements

Poetry comes from a lifetime of input, so covering every debt would take a volume. Yet I do want to express appreciation to a number of specific stimuli: to the Silver Age of DC comics and the work of Carmine Infantino, Sidney Greene, Dick Sprang, Wayne Boring, Gardner Fox, and, of course, Julius Schwartz; to Mac Raboy and Harry Harrison for their definitive (to me) depiction of Flash Gordon; to Kenji Tsuruta's *Spirit of Wonder* (obviously behind "The Birthday Moon"); to Ian McDonald in *New Moon* for introducing me to "saudade"; to the folklore and mythology of the Native-American Pacific Northwest, the Navajo, and the Aboriginal Australians; to the TV and film productions of *Rocky Jones, Tom Corbett*, and *The Forbidden Planet*; to the map of Krypton in the first *Superman Annual*; to my friends, colleagues, mentors, and teachers (Paul Goat Allen, Michael Arnzen, Timons Esaias, Johanna Gribble, Lee McClain, Heidi Ruby Miller, Harry Mooney, Richard O'Keefe, Nicole Peeler), to the many children of Jamie and Paul; and to all the great writers of SF and poetry who've inspired me (Poul Anderson, William Blake, Lord Byron, Arthur Clarke, T. S. Eliot, Peter Hamilton, Andre Norton, Michael Ondaatje, Clifford Simak, Dan Simmons, Wallace Stevens—to mention just a few!).

And, of course, many thanks to Jennifer Barnes and John Edward Lawson at Dog Star Books for so wonderfully supporting my efforts, to Bradley Sharp for yet one more sensational cover, and finally to Carol, for just being alive, and for being her thoughtful, kind, and always close-when-needed self. All of you are here in some obvious or hidden way, and I hope I've provided a worthy reflection.

About the Author

Albert Wendland has made a career out of his lifelong interests in science fiction—and photography, art, film, and travel. He teaches popular fiction, literature, and writing at Seton Hill University, where, from 2008 to 2015, he was director of its MFA in Writing Popular Fiction (the program famous for its exclusive attention to genre writing). His SF novel, *The Man Who Loved Alien Landscapes*, was a starred pick-of-the-week by *Publisher's Weekly*, and the prequel, *In a Suspect Universe*, was published in 2018, describing a story from the protagonist's past. He's also written and published a book-length study of science fiction, a chapter in *Many Genres, One Craft*, a poem in *Drawn to Marvel: Poems from the Comic Books*, and several articles on SF and writing. He enjoys landscape photography, astronomy, graphic novels, and the "sublime."

www.ingramcontent.com/pod-product-compliance
Lightning Source LLC
Chambersburg PA
CBHW020634250626
47154CB00008B/2669